LOVE-LIES-BLEEDING

LOVE-LIES-BLEEDING

Lex Vern

iUniverse, Inc.
New York Lincoln Shanghai

Love-Lies-Bleeding

iUniverse books may be ordered through booksellers or by contacting:

iUniverse
2021 Pine Lake Road, Suite 100
Lincoln, NE 68512
www.iuniverse.com
1-800-Authors (1-800-288-4677)

ISBN-13: 978-0-595-39152-3 (pbk)
ISBN-13: 978-0-595-83538-6 (ebk)
ISBN-10: 0-595-39152-4 (pbk)
ISBN-10: 0-595-83538-4 (ebk)

Printed in the United States of America

CHAPTER 1

The question of how I started in my line of work was frequently presented to me. For some reason, most people seem to think that being molested as a child, having been raped or having been through some form of abuse is somewhat a prerequisite of becoming a stripper or to be politically correct, "exotic dancer." Well neither one of those choices fit my profile so before I go on, I think it wise to tell you how I got started.

As an only child, I, Samantha Leanne Goldsmith, was born and raised by a single parent, my father, Leonard, in Savannah, Georgia. My mother died giving birth to me so as far as I can remember, I've always been my father's most precious prize. He worked for the Post Office since before I was born. When he wasn't working you could always find the both of us either at church or on the ten-acre farm that was left to him by my grandfather. Daddy was known around town for his homegrown vegetables and I, for my well-kept flower garden. So as dad worked the farm, I would be on the side of the house tending to our flowers. Daddy always joked around about how my corner lot had grown into a perimeter lot or how my flowers seemed to take over his vegetables but I knew he loved having me out there with him. On Saturday afternoons he'd watch me from the front porch picking out the flowers that were usually used for the centerpiece of the church podium. You could see the joy and how proud Daddy was when Rev. Myers would give a special thank you for the beautiful flowers to me, Sammie Lea (the name that I've been stuck with from Samantha Leanne) for the beautiful flowers.

Over the years these acres had been a bond between dad and me. Working the land was the one place where we were both at peace; the place where we didn't have to talk to each other to feel connected and the one thing we were both passionate about. Even with his tight schedule, he still managed to be very active in the local church and controlled every second of my waking life. Not that I didn't appreciate him caring for me God knows I loved him for that but he had a way of being in my space and making me claustrophobic sometimes. I guess that was the price of being an only child.

I didn't have many friends, so the older couples or widows that he and mom grew up with by default, became my friends. Since everything I did usually involved my dad, my only source of freedom came from going to school, being part of the dance team, and tending to my flowers. Living in a place where the most exciting event was gossip spread during prayer meetings on Monday nights, you tend to wonder what life was all about at a very early age. I knew I wanted to get away from this one-mule town so getting good grades was always one of my priorities. No matter what happened, I had to get accepted to a major university far away from home.

My senior year came and went by fast but not fast enough. Every week or so dad would sit me down and question me about my goals in life. To be truthful I think he just wanted to make sure that I saw things his way and wanted to be a lawyer. From the time I was a kid I told him how I wanted to be a dance teacher but the idea was enough to kill. He'd always tell me how he never had a chance to finish college and become a lawyer so being his only child; he was hoping I'd carry on the dream. Of course, I still thought about dancing but over the years, however, dad have convinced me that becoming a lawyer was more prestigious and would provide broader avenues to help people and, of course, make lots of money. He would always say, "A lawyer can go dancing anytime but a dance teacher cannot be a lawyer whenever he or she wants."

When my college acceptance letters arrived, my father would often whine about how far the school was. So, when I finally received my acceptance letter from University of Miami, home of the "Hurricanes," I thought I won the lottery. It was far enough from Savannah yet close enough for dad in comparison to the schools in California, Washington State or New York.

On the day I was scheduled to leave Savannah, Georgia, my father woke up to fix breakfast. I was so excited, I never even slept but looking at him in the kitchen you could tell he was dying inside and for the first time I actually felt bad about leaving him. Of course, he had lots of friends but it's not like he could control them like he does me. The bottom line was he was losing his little girl. We got to the University of Miami early afternoon; my room appeared empty which indicated that my roommate wasn't there yet. We got my stuff in and decided to start unpacking as dad went out to find a hotel for the two nights he was gonna be in town.

The first couple days of orientation, dad and I went back and forth between school offices, the mall, bookstores, and restaurants. The day he was to leave for Savannah Georgia, we stood in front of the University waiting for a cab to take him to the airport. As we waited, we talked about my classes and according to dad, went over some last minute safety guidelines needed by all college freshman. Before I knew it, the Yellow Cab was there waiting. As we hugged and said goodbye, I found myself crying. Then my father surprised me even more when he told me how proud he was of me then handed me a small booklet with some of our favorite flowers pressed throughout the pages. As we wiped off my tears he said, "This way, our garden will always be a page away when things get tough."

My freshmen year went by smoothly. My roommate, unlike me, was from New York City. I was pre-law; she was pre-med. The first few weeks in school we barely exchanged a word but after the tryout for the dance team, we were the only two freshmen who made the team. As Hurricanettes, pretty soon we were inseparable. When I called dad to tell him about being a Hurricanette he didn't fail to remind me how I needed to stay focused and couldn't afford to mess up my grades. I know he'd rather I join some law club but I couldn't get dancing totally out of my head. Besides there was no harm in being in a dance team while I studied to become a lawyer.

Sophomore year was also a blast. Jessica and I discovered the University of Miami college life of "boys, beer and parties." My relationships never got further than going out or first base because there were so many guys to choose from. Besides, it was my way of staying out of trouble unlike Jessica who, as she puts it, was exploring her sexual realm. As much as I used to think that the people from my church in Savannah were old fashioned for their "saving yourself until marriage or the body being the Lord's temple" kind of talk, I could look around the campus and see their point. Don't get me wrong, I still think they're old fashioned and somewhat hypocritical considering a lot of them ignored those same rules growing up but these boys down here were ruthless. They'd sleep with a girl today and give it a couple of days, the whole school would know about it. Or you'd see a couple supposedly in love and two weeks later she's crying because her boyfriend cheated on her. It's not that I was better than these girls, I just had enough sense to know that none of these boys were going to get some from me. At first they tried but having grown up around an older man, I was way ahead of their games. Those were the times when I would thank dad and his corny friends for letting me know what was up.

With me being into sports and playful, I was soon known as one of the guys and with my charming looks, the guys didn't mind having me around. Some of the guys would sometimes say, "If you'd stop being so playful, we might take the time to see how pretty you are," but I figure why ruin a good thing. I was getting as many dates as the next girl without giving up my body.

Spring break of my junior year, my father came to visit instead of me going home. We drove around for the three days visiting some of the hot spots of Miami, restaurants and even the malls. In the midst of all the fun, something seemed to be wrong with daddy. Every now and then I'd catch him lost in thought or staring into space. Something was clearly bothering him.

CHAPTER 2

Summertime came along and I landed an internship at a local law firm and got a part-time job to help out with the expenses. One afternoon coming back from the office, I went back to my room to change into my work clothes when I noticed the note with my name on the door: "Urgent—Call Dr. Houston (912) 555-2000." I stood there staring at the note trying to make sense out of it, then I recognized the Georgia area code. I opened the door and rushed to the phone, the whole time thinking of daddy.

"Savannah Memorial," said the lady's voice on the other end. "Hello my name is Samantha Goldsmith, I'm returning Dr. Houston's call. "Just a moment please." A minute or two went by before the doctor finally picked up the line. "Miss Goldsmith?" "Yes," I answered with fear in my voice. "We have your father at the hospital and from what he told us you're his only family. Is there anyway you could make it up here?" "Can you tell me what happened?...What's wrong with him." "I think it's best we discuss all that when you get here," said the doctor. "I'll be there tomorrow."

Right before noon I made it to Savannah and took a taxi straight to the hospital. The front desk gave me the room number on the fourth floor. I walked into the room to find a man apparently sleeping with all kinds of machines, tubes and wires attached to him from head to toe. I rushed back outside to read the name on the wall and sure enough I was in the right room. Oh my goodness, my father was not even recognizable! I went back inside and moved up near his head, and saw that he was asleep. I wanted to hug him so bad but all I could do was cry. I sat on the empty bed across from him and everything, yet nothing was going through my mind. I looked up to see the doctor who was just walking in:

"Miss Goldsmith?" he asked. "Yes," I said, as I attempted to clean my face with some tissue. "Come, let's talk somewhere else, we don't want to wake him up." As I sat in the empty waiting room, I listened to the doctor telling me about my father's condition. As my mind wandered in confusion unwilling to deal with this reality, he went over the various medications and treatments my father had been on then he hit me with the words that I was so afraid to hear. "He's in real bad shape," the doctor said, "he didn't want us to call you but things don't look too favorable this time so we thought it best for you to be here." "This time? What do you mean? Has this happened before?" "I'm sorry, Miss Goldsmith, but your father has had two previous heart attacks, neither one of them had been this serious but nevertheless..." "Is there any hope?" I interrupted "There's surgery," he replied, "but it all depends on how soon he recovers from the stroke."

The doctor thought my dad was too weak to undergo surgery. The idea of my father being weak could not fit in my brain; but that was the reality of things and I was gonna have to deal with it.

Back in the room, I went back to the empty bed across from dad's. He looked so weak and helpless. Part of me wished he was awake just to ask him why, why did he keep this from me? The other part of me just wanted him to rest and I wanted to hug him and take this away from him. My thoughts began to drift away when I heard him cough. His eyes opened wide as he realized I was in the room. I moved close to the bed to give him a hello kiss. I took his right hand in mine and for a moment with a big smile on his face he just stared at me as he gathered his strength to speak:

"How was the flight?" he asked. "How are you?" I replied, wanting to bring him back to what we needed to talk about. "I'm sorry you have to see me like this" he said. "Shu...shu." "It's okay," I said, "I'm sorry you have to go through this." We talked about his condition, the treatments he's been through, the doctor's advice, etc. Daddy was barely above a whisper and from time to time he would stop to catch his breath. I could tell that talking for so long was a real chore for him. Soon after, the doctor walked in and informed us of that daddy was schedule for an MRI and a slew of other tests. As much as I wanted to go with him to the testing area, the doctor would not let me. Since the process would take most of the afternoon, I decided to go home, freshen up, and come back for the night.

When the taxi dropped me off in front of our empty house on Whitmore Place, it was about 2:00 P.M. The emptiness of the three-bedroom house made it seem larger than what it was. I cleaned up a little, became hungry and found a can of Campbell's chicken noodle soup which was gonna have to do for now. I called my roommate back in Miami, let her know what was going on and promised to keep her posted on how things turned out.

The next few days seemed to be the longest days of my life. Every time dad would seem to be doing better, something would go wrong and we'd be back to square one again. It was really discouraging and at times I could almost see him wanting to give up. I'd try to cheer him up but many times I would fail at the task. His left side was completely nonfunctioning; he was in so much pain sometimes that cheering him up would seem uncaring. All I could and would do was hold his hand and let him know I was there. A week went by unnoticed. Many of the church people came by to visit and pray and some of dad's friends would often come by in the afternoon to check on him. The few painless moments he had we'd spend them looking through my pressed flower booklet reminiscing over the tales and memories that were laid throughout the pages. Thursday of my second week in Savannah, I walked in Daddy's room with a bag holding stuff that daddy wanted me to bring from the house. I also brought a few blankets since I was going to spend the night at the hospital. The doctors and the nurses were kind enough to tolerate me going in and out at all hours of the day and night so the empty bed in daddy's room had became familiar to me. I pulled out the set of cards from the bag, set the blankets on the opposite bed and set an old picture of my mother next to daddy's bed. I don't know why he wanted that particular picture but it took me at least an hour to find it in his room. After eating his hospital dinner we played cards and talked about my mother. Daddy rarely talked about mom and the few things I knew about my mother were from grandma before she passed. Daddy went on about how pretty she was, how I reminded him of her, stories of my younger days, some old and some new. It was probably the most dad and I ever talked since I've left for school. He asked me about my plans for the future as if he didn't know and how school was going. As much as I was enjoying this moment, there was a sense of uneasiness in the air but at the same time I was happy to see him talk because he had been in so much pain the past few days that even eating was impossible for him. His left side including the left part of his face was completely out of commission, which made it hard to understand some of his words. We were silent for a while when out of the blue he asked me, "Sammie Lee, do you really want to be a lawyer?" "Dad, what kind of a question is that, I only have one more year before law school." "Sammie Lee," he said in his impeded speech "you didn't answer the question." "Okay," I said with a smirk on my face "the answer is yes and you've seen my grades which I'm sure speaks for itself."

He placed his cards down, took my hands in his only functioning hand and said, "Whatever you do…make sure you're happy, you hear me baby girl." "Yes daddy."

He became tired from all the talking and soon after, the nurse came in for his medication. That night, I sat next to him reading a book and thinking about our conversation. I hadn't thought about becoming a lawyer thing in such a long time. Once my major was selected I just made it a point to keep my grades up and as long as daddy was happy, I was happy. Around 11:00 P.M. I was just about to drift into sleep when he grabbed my hand again. I opened my eyes and looked at him and he asked me for a goodnight kiss. I smiled and thought him silly for a moment and then I reached, kissed him on his forehead and gave him a gentle hug as not to hurt him or disturb the multiple wires connected to him. After hugging him, he was smiling into sleep. That was the last time I saw him smile. When the heart monitor suddenly woke me up that night, daddy and his smile were gone. I sat there on the bed, looking at him, and then I hugged him. I wanted to cry, I wanted to scream, but at the same time it's as if an inner strength had taken over me and no sound would come out. He had suffered so much I didn't know which was worst, having him here suffering or being gone.

Before I knew it the room was filled with nurses and doctors. I moved back letting them get to him. The wires and the machines were pulled away from him and soon after the room was empty again. I moved to his bed resting my head on his chest and cried. "You can't leave me yet," I cried, "you can't leave me, you can't leave me." But he did. At 55 years old, he was gone, leaving me with not a soul in the world on Thursday July 30th. I was now an orphan.

My next big task was dealing with the funeral arrangements. Here I was barely nineteen having to deal with this situation. Where do I start? How and what was I supposed to do? One of the doctors came in asking me to follow him to the office. Sitting at the table were some of the doctors that had worked on my dad, the insurance representative and the social worker. They went over the pile of papers that needed to be signed while I sat unaware of what they were talking about. My father just died for goodness sake, how could they expect me to be in my right mind to sign papers? As if they couldn't wait. I guess everyone was trying to cover their ass. I signed whatever they wanted me to, just to get away from them.

They asked me if I had chosen a funeral home but, of course, I hadn't reached that point yet. This went on for at least 20 minutes, which seemed like forever to me. Finally, everyone was gone except for the social worker, she offered to help me with the arrangements since she understood I was alone. She gave me my dad's file including his insurance papers, which, of course, I was clueless about. I called a funeral home and they told me they'd be there within the next half hour. When I walked back in the room, he was already covered from head to toe. I sat at the end of the bed in tears with our pressed flower booklet, the last thing he held in his hand. While waiting for the funeral home to get to the hospital, I looked at dad for the last time as if to make sure he was really dead and as my fingers traced over the Amaranths, his favorite flower, I could hear him say "Your garden will always be a page away when things get tough."

I drove home in dad's old Dodge pick-up truck and as soon as I walked through the door, the only thing I could do was cry. It's funny how as much as I didn't want to be bothered with anybody I wished I had someone that at least I could turn to in case I chose to do so but there was no one. No family, no parents, no friends.

Hours went by and I must have fallen asleep right on the floor. It was 1:00 o'clock Friday afternoon when the pounding on the door woke me up. I looked through the window to see who it was and there stood Rev. Myers the minister from dad's church with three of the church ladies. They came in and told me how they'd just heard the news and how sorry they were. It never seems to amaze me how fast news can travel in a small town. One way or another they'd find out if you were dead or alive. Well, it was thoughtful of them and the gesture was appreciated. They gave me their numbers in case I needed anything and they were gone.

With the help of the church and the social worker I managed to give dad a decent farewell. And on August 5th 1993, my father was laid to rest next to my mother whom I've never known.

Some of the people I knew from high school showed up at the funeral. After the burial, Mr. and Mrs. Greene, one of dad's oldest and closest friends, hosted a luncheon at their place for all of dad's friends. I hung around all afternoon shaking hands, hugging and kissing people that dropped by to pay their respects. It was getting late and reaching the time where I didn't want to be bothered with anyone anymore but Mrs. Greene insisted that I spend a couple of days with them until I felt better. And how long did she think that was going to be? I know these small town people meant well but I really didn't want to be around a bunch of people who felt sorry for me. Just out of respect I agreed to spend the night and told her I'd have to go back home in the morning and start getting things in order.

The first few weeks after the funeral were painful. All I could do was cry. People came by to visit the first few days after but then it was just me and the occasional visit from Mrs. Greene and Reverend Myers. The house needed to be cleaned, a lot of stuff had to be thrown away and I had to start thinking about getting back to Miami.

Three weeks went by and I barely had one of the rooms cleaned out. Daddy must have kept every piece of paper under the sun. I spent days going through files, boxes, bags and I had just as much left to go through. I had to decide what I was going to do with the house. There were still more papers for me to sign from the funeral home, bills from the hospital and insurance claim papers. There was just so much I had to figure out on my own.

CHAPTER 3

My roommate Jessica called and told me that a major hurricane was supposed to hit Miami. Well everybody knows South Florida is a hurricane magnet and most of the residents usually go through the season without paying much attention to it. She told me of all the warnings that were issued, and how people had to evacuate from their homes.

As predicted, Hurricane Andrew came through and made a big mess out of the city. People were killed, homes and business were destroyed, electricity was out, and I could go on and on. All this went on without me even knowing. I guess it'd been a while since I turned on the TV. The university like most business in South Florida was closed until further notice due to damages. I later called my job to find out they got destroyed, which also meant I no longer had a job. It was just a part time job but still it helped and dad wasn't around anymore to help me out. I definitely was gonna have to find something when I got back. For now I had "Georgia on my mind" I had to get the house ready for whatever I was gonna do with it.

Two months after the funeral, I locked up the house, hopped into daddy's Dodge pick-up truck and headed back to Miami. The city looked a lot worse than I expected. Obviously this hurricane was no joke. The streets were still dirty and even though it had been weeks since the hurricane had gone through, electrical poles and wires were still on the ground, and trees were still blocking some intersections, drinking water and electricity were yet to be restored, many people were telling me how much worse things were the few weeks before. I went to register for my classes and found out that I'd miss the deadline for my scholarship. I called dad's accountant only to learn that my college fund account had been dried out since last year. I couldn't even apply for a loan until I had the results from my Pell grants. I went ahead and registered by faith hoping things would work out one-way or another.

Two weeks into school I found out that my Pell grant barely covered half of my tuition. Without a co-signer I couldn't qualify for a loan so unless I was able to come up with some money, I had to move out of the dorm. I had some money left in the bank but I had to buy my books, eat and put gas in my car if I was going to look for a job. Where was I going to go? I had no family in Miami or anywhere in the state that I knew of and here I was with only a week to figure out where I was going to go. Once my week was up, I spent the next couple of weeks sneaking in friends' rooms, spending the night and buying some time until I was able to find a job. With the loss of my dad still fresh on my mind everything else seemed minimal in comparison.

Finding a job in Miami had never been so hard. With the mess left from the hurricanes most jobs were closed or destroyed. Thousands of construction companies were hiring but with 120 lbs. on my 5'7" body and no experience, who would hire me? This was not the type of job where being cute mattered and the few entry-level jobs available came along with a Spanish-speaking requirement. The classified section of the Miami Herald was becoming my best reading material. Every day after school I would drive around looking for jobs and…nothing. My dad's insurance money was used for medical bills and his funeral. What was left over was used for my getting back to Miami leaving me with $1,500 deposited in my account and buying books took up most of that. Things were not looking too bright for me in the Sunshine state. I spent my nights crying and at times I'd ask myself whether I was crying because of my situation or because dad was gone. Either way I had plenty of reasons to cry.

Jessica moved back to New York and dropped out of college so I was left with no real friends. I called her once in a while but with everything going on in my life I couldn't keep up with her. People that I knew were constantly telling me how I had to be strong, that things were going to be okay. Half the time I wanted to tell them to go to hell, what did they think I was doing, being weak?

Spending the night at my friends' wasn't working out too well. They were all sharing rooms with other people so they could only put me up for so long. As far as my male friends were concerned, I didn't trust them enough to crash in their rooms; even if I was "one of the boys." By late November, I knew I'd reached rock bottom. I had the starless sky view of the city, $40.00 in pocket, and everything I owned was bagged up in a hefty garbage bag on the floor of dad's Dodge pick-up truck. My thoughts were wandering around trying to find a way out of my situation. I needed something, anything that could clear my mind or make my problems go away if only for a while but drugs and alcohol were not my thing and therefore not an option. The few friends I had helped me as much as they could, and God was making his way down my shit list. One may think me mad for saying such a thing about God but what had I done that was so bad that I had to be punished for? Yet here I was homeless, unemployed and almost out of school.

Tired of feeling sorry for myself I drove to a near by 7-Eleven to grab a bite to eat. I was walking by the entrance door when a classified ad from last week caught my attention. "Dancers wanted $200.00 or more a shift. No experience necessary. Call anytime between 12:00 P.M. to 5:00 A.M." How could I have missed this ad? Of course, I was no Baryshnikov, but dancing had always been one of my passions; besides, between my high school dance team and being a Hurricanette I figured I had enough experience to at least tryout.

It was about 11:00 P.M. when I looked at the ad again and realized that this ad wasn't the kind of place that required the skills of Baryshnikov; this was probably a strip bar. Although I'd never been to one, some of the guys from college have shared stories of their visits to local the strip bars.

A few days went by and the idea kept running through my head. I knew of all the reasons why I shouldn't even think about the idea but at the same time I couldn't think of an alternate solution. A week later, with my money running out and my job prospects non-existent, I decided to call. I talked to someone at the place and scheduled an appointment for the next day at 4:00 P.M.

It took me about an hour to get to my appointment due to the traffic lights not working in most parts of Miami. It was funny how certain parts of Miami seemed so foreign to me. I got to the right place, parked the truck, grabbed my bag and rushed through the door at 3:45. As I opened the door, the darkness swallowed up the light coming from the outside. A man with arms twice the size of my thighs stood behind a cornered counter in the hallway, which separated the entrance from the main room. After telling him whom I was here to see, he escorted me to an office where Larry, the manager, was sitting behind a desk. I was so nervous that the cigarette smell and the darkness that seemed to be all over the place went unnoticed.

Larry was an older man with a full gray mixed beard and a beer belly, which strangely enough, added a certain charisma to his look. He was on the phone when I walked in, so the guy from the front door pointed to a chair for me to sit in and immediately left the room. Larry covered the receiver and told me he'd be with me soon. The room was nothing I would imagine for an office.

Cases of wine, beer, champagne, whiskey and rum; it reminded me of a liquor store. The bottles occupied half of the office from floor up and on the other half sat the big desk where Larry was seated. To the right of the two office chairs on part of the wall were pictures of beer advertisements and girls in bikinis followed by a metal shelf, which held three small televisions that obviously were connected to cameras. I started wondering about the place, wondering what I was doing, but before I could finish my thoughts, Larry placed the receiver down and started to address me:

"Hi, I'm Larry. You're the girl I spoke to yesterday?" "Yes sir, I…" "Are you over 18?" "Yes, I'm 19, I'll be 20 in eight months." I wasn't sure whether he was taking notes, or working on something else while he was talking to me, but he seemed to be writing something. He went on with the meaningless questions then at his request, I stood up and turned around a couple of times. He looked at me from head to toe then told me I was hired. "Thank you sir," I replied "but don't you um, um," clearing my throat "don't you want me to audition?" "Nah, you have the body and the face, you'll do just fine" was Larry's response.

The afternoon shift had just started so Larry invited me to the bar to grab a drink and watch the girls to get an idea of how things worked. "Some time tomorrow we'll have to make you a schedule," he said as we exited the office. I followed him to the bar as I listened to his explanation of how the scheduling worked. He told me that I was free to pick my shift as long as I worked at least three days out of the week. I walked through the darkness of the club and for the first time since I entered this unknown place I could absorb my surrounding. The large rectangular room was divided into three sections. On the far right, was the well stacked circular bar, about ten feet to the right were the doors to the office storage room, followed by the bathrooms and the girls' dressing room. A well-lit stage surrounded by a black counter top was situated in the center. The stage was elevated about two feet from the ground with a brass pole on the side, black elevated stools lined around the counter giving it a miniature bar setting. A few customers were sitting with their drinks and a waitress wearing all black was tending to them. On the far left was a glass brick room known as the Champagne Room followed by a few private booths with silver glittered curtains preventing the inside from being seen and then I noticed the DJ's booth which was up high on a platform to give him a clear view of every corner of the club. Small round tables with matching chairs were scattered all around filling in the rest of the room.

Two middle-aged men sitting at the entrance to the bar called to Larry as we approached the bar. Larry introduced me to them as the new girl. We shook hands, Larry proceeded to request a beer for him and instructed the bartender to get me whatever I wanted. Since the music in the room overpowered the conversations, I was clueless of what they were talking about. After getting his drink, Larry told me to let him know if I needed anything, excused himself and all three men got up and followed him to the office. Sitting at the bar, I faced the stage where a topless girl with a cowboy hat and high-heeled cowboy boots was dancing to an Allen Jackson song. I knew I had to leave this place, but before I could get off the burgundy-cushioned stool the bartender's voice behind me made me turn around:

"Hi, I'm Karen. Are you gonna have anything to drink?" "A Coke, please." "Just plain Coke?" She yelled back as if to make sure she heard me right. "Yes please." Karen came back with the drink and placed it on the counter, but by then the only place I wanted to be was in my car driving away from this place. I stood up and asked Karen to tell Larry that something came up and that I had to go. I had no idea I could walk so fast, but minutes later I was on my way to South Beach. My thoughts were running faster than my car, and my situation seemed like it was only getting worse by the minute.

A few weeks went by and my search for a job remained unsuccessful. Sometimes at night, I would watch the people sleeping on the sidewalks and think back on times when I'd wondered how and why so many people were homeless. Now I was one of them. As I laid across the seat in the truck, I tried to pray and ask for help but I felt too empty, perhaps because of my resentment towards God. I kept thinking of the club but I just couldn't picture myself taking my clothes off in front of total strangers. So much went through my mind from going back to Georgia to suicide, but deep down I knew these were not the answers. Going back to Georgia would be like giving up on daddy and on myself. I made a promise to daddy that I was gonna be a lawyer and make something of myself. I came to Miami for that reason and somehow, someway, I had to make it happen.

CHAPTER 4

Before I knew it I had $10.00 left to my name. I was forced to leave school and still had no job, no place to live and not much to do except feel sorry for myself. My whole world seemed to be sinking away into some unknown dimension. I was parked in a vacant parking lot by the beach about to fall asleep one night when a sharp cry brought me back. I picked up my head and saw a man trying to pull a girl out of a car. The dim streetlights reflected on the broken glass on the floor indicated that some of the windows had been shattered. I waited for a while thinking of how I could help then decided to go to a pay phone to call the police. Before I could find my keys, I watched them drive away. The inside of the truck was lighted by the moonlight, and I caught sight of the old classified page with the dancing ad that I had been looking at for the past few weeks. I looked out my windows, but nothing could be seen. I made sure my doors were locked (as if that was going to make a difference) in case someone wanted get to me and turn to the ad again with my tired eyes. I stared at it while thinking of all the reasons why I couldn't and shouldn't go back to the club. Things like what dad's reaction would be if he was still alive, how this could affect my career later on? That night, I decided not to think of reasons, or how scared I was. I knew I had to survive somehow, and living in my car wasn't going to cut it for long. I needed to get back in school and I was tired of sleeping with one eye open while expecting the worst. I picked up the ad, and before even realizing what I was doing, I was driving down the street to the gas station, going to a pay phone to call Larry. As I drove I pleaded and apologized out loud to daddy and to myself. "I'm sorry, I'm so sorry, but I don't know what else to do. I'll make it up to you daddy, I'll make it up to you, I'll make you proud, I promise I will" I kept babbling those words out loud as I pushed back the tears that were ready to come out. It was almost midnight when I called, so Larry told me to come the next day for the night shift, which started at 8:00 P.M.

The lights around the club's name, Unicorn, were flashing on and off. When I pulled in, I carried in a bag packed with my only black heels, two bras with matching panties, and a white long sleeve dress shirt that I'd kept from daddy's closet. The same guy, who turned out to be the bouncer, was at the door again and Karen, the bartender, was behind the bar talking to Larry. After a quick hello Larry took me to the dressing room. He briefly introduced me to the eight or nine girls that were sitting in front of the mirrored wall then walked out the door. Some of the girls were smoking and others drinking. Apart from the blonde flipping through a magazine wearing jeans and a t-shirt, they were all day shift girls who were just finishing up. They were all wearing high heels and had their money attached to a garter band around their thighs. From the looks of it, some of them had a little too much to drink. After some minor make-up and hair touch-ups, they evacuated the dressing room.

Suddenly I felt so alone, I knew I had to get ready, but I didn't know where or how to start. I pulled out my make-up bag and as I stared into the mirror I felt the hot tears making their way down my face. I was trying to stop my tears, but they had a mind of their own:

"Is this your first time dancing?"

I was startled by the voice and looked up to see the blonde in the jeans. She was sitting in the corner of the long rectangular room holding her magazine. "I'm sorry," I said, "I thought I was alone." "That's okay," she said approaching the empty stools next to me. "My name is Deedee, what's yours?" "Samantha," I said. "Is that your stage name?" By the look on my face it was obvious that I didn't know what Deedee was talking about. She pulled a cigarette from the pack she held in her hand and offered one to me. To this I politely decline. "Don't worry," said Deedee. "I'll be more than happy to clue you into this place. You really shouldn't use your real name, so we first have to find you a stage name. Let's see…what would be a suitable name for you?" As if talking to herself, she said, "Angel. You have that innocent and angelic look, so Angel will work just fine. Now we need make-up, costumes, heels and a garter. By the end of the night, you'll see that it's not that bad. Besides, it's almost Christmas, and it's Friday. Not crying day but payday! There's lots of money to be made tonight."

Deedee was trying to cheer me up. Without an invitation she started telling me about her first time dancing. As she talked, she looked at the stuff that I was pulling out of my bag then she walked to her locker aligned with others by the dressing room door. Inside the tall and narrow locker, costumes of all different colors could be seen. She picked a short white silk negligee with matching garter belt and handed them to me. I was a little reluctant since I wanted to wear my own stuff, but somehow Deedee persuaded me otherwise.

"Think about it," she said. "If these men wanted to see girls in plain underclothes they would have gone home to their wives. They want to see something different and sexy. You know…out of the ordinary. I had to admit, Deedee made sense and so I took the outfit from her hands. She headed for the door as she told me to think of the type of music I wanted to dance to so she could tell the DJ. I put the negligee on and through my teary eyes, I had to admit that it fit me perfectly. I stared into the mirror, trying to make sense out of everything; I knew I didn't want to be here, but I didn't know how to get myself out of what I was getting into. Deedee came back with a small tray containing one Long Island Ice Tea and four shots of Tequila. She took a shot. Then, as I went on with my makeup, Deedee talked about the do's and don't s of the business:

"There's a way of doing everything, and being a stripper is no different. You always take care of your bartenders, because they have control of your drinks. The more you drink, the more you sell. The more you sell, the more money you make on commissions. If you don't feel like drinking, let the bartender know in advance so she can give you non-alcoholic drinks. Never turn down a drink and never let the customer know if your drink is a virgin. The drunker the customer thinks you are, the more money he will spend. When you go on stage you'll dance to a two-song set, by the end of the second song you should be completely nude. After your sets, you go around the club and collect your tips. If a customer asks for a private dance, it's $10.00 minimum per song. No touching allowed. If a customer gives you a problem, let Jason or Eric know and they'll take care of it. That's their job as bouncers. At the end of the night, the DJ gets 10% of whatever you make and the bartender and bouncers get whatever you think is reasonable."

It felt like I was taking a crash course. I was trying to calm my nerves as I listened to Deedee, but I knew I couldn't remember all the stuff that she was throwing at me. One would think she had a Ph.D. in the field.

"How long have you been dancing?"

"Almost eight years," she said. "I started when I was 17." For a split moment Deedee was quiet, then she took a shot off of the tray, threw it down her throat, and handed one to me. As she bit on her lime, she realized that I hadn't touched mine. "Believe it or not, some girls are born for this place." Deedee went on with a serious look on her face. "They can walk in and take off their clothes with no problems. Some will even go the extra mile and let the customers have their way with them for an extra buck or two. You, mama, don't seem to be one of those girls. Just try the shots and maybe you'll stop shaking so we can go on the floor and make some money. One last thing, if you need some help taking your clothes off when you get on stage, pretend you're about to have the best sex of your life." "I've never had sex before." I found myself saying out loud. Deedee did a double take. Realizing I was for real, she let out a sympathetic laugh. "Girl, what are you doing here? You don't drink?" "I drink beer," I said in a matter-of-fact sort of way. She gave me this "whatever" look and went on "you've never been fucked, and you probably don't smoke either, do you?" "No," I answered to her last statement. "You have two choices," she said. "Get a few shots down so you can do this, or leave now." She handed me two shots of Tequila and pushed the Long Island Ice Tea towards me.

The D.J. came in to make a list of my music selections and told me I would go on stage after Deedee, who was four girls away from her turn. The dressing room slowly filled up with girls for the evening shift. By the time Deedee was finished getting ready, I had put away two shots of Tequila, and was slowly working on the Long Island Ice Tea, all of which were taking effect very quickly.

My first time on stage was one of the most frightening moments in my life. Both songs went by and the white silk mini-lingerie was sitting on my evenly spread hips. I knew I had to take it all off, but once my well-sloped 34-B breasts were exposed, I just couldn't go all the way. All I could hear was the voices of my father and his fellow churchgoers back home talking about the 'purity of the body'. Oh! The thoughts and vision of my father turning over in his grave and coming back to kick my butt for doing what he would call the 'unthinkable.' As I stood on the stage, I looked at the eyes around the room, and I could feel my shame as they violated me. The rest of the night went without me knowing. I couldn't remember how much I had to drink or even how I got to my car.

The sun had been out for a while, and I had no idea what time it was when I woke up Saturday morning in my car at a Shell gas station. My head was pounding and my stomach was begging for food. I strolled in and asked the cashier for the nearest hotel. A Comfort Inn was half a mile from where I was. On my way to the hotel, I stopped at a McDonald's to grab a bite. I knew I had made some money, but when I opened my bag to pay for the food, I was shocked at the sight of the pile of bills staring at me. I had no recollection of the night let alone how much money I made.

After checking in, I carried my bags to the room but before I could make use of the inviting queen size bed, my face had to meet the toilet bowl. Everything from McDonald's came up along with whatever I had the night before. The strong smell of the cigarettes, vomit, and alcohol reminded me of how badly I needed a shower, but I was too anxious to know how much money I had actually made. I poured the bills out of my bag and onto the bed after counting the money at least three times; I had $624.00 staring at me.

Forgetting about my headache, I jumped up and down with joy like a kid at the sight of a newfound treasure. I tried to catch my breath and calm down then caught a glimpse of myself in the mirror attached to the dresser. I didn't look like I was in pain, apart from my headache; I wasn't hungry. For the first time in months I had a bed to sleep in, yet tears flowed down my face. I looked in the mirror and felt betrayed by no other than myself. I looked at the money on the bed, then back to my reflection, and the feeling I had felt on stage was suddenly back; shameful and violated. I ran into the shower with tears in my eyes. The soaping and scrubbing went on for what seemed like forever, and as the headache persisted, I dried off and found my way to the bed in search for some comfort.

I woke up with a sharp pain in my stomach and lucky enough I was able to make it to the bathroom just in time. I vomited whatever was left in my system. When I finally stopped, my head seemed to spin in all directions. I hugged the toilet for a while until I was able to stand and wash my face. When I finally made it back to the bed, the clock read "7:00 P.M." I had slept the entire day. I wanted to sleep some more, for my body was tired after working until 5:00 AM but I knew I had to try to eat something since my stomach was completely empty. I called out for pizza, laid back down, and waited.

CHAPTER 5

I booked my room for another three days at $60.00 a day, thinking that would be sufficient time to figure out what I had to do. My only choices were: find a job, go back to the club, or use the money to buy a ticket and move back to Savannah. Moving back was out of the question, so that left me with finding a job, which would take a miracle or the club, which still made me uneasy. The three days went by and yet my decisions were still uncertain, I checked out and drove to the beach for some fresh air and change of scenery.

The sun was setting when I decided to go look for a cheap motel for the night. I pulled in a Subway store along the way to get some food and joined the waiting line that was moving slowly.

"Hi, Angel" I heard a voice call out from behind. My mind was elsewhere so the noise in my stomach and the voice behind me blended right along with the surrounding noise. I moved a step closer to the counter and turned around as I felt a hand on my shoulder. "Angel, what are you doing around here?" It was Deedee, the girl from the club, standing behind me. I was wondering why she was calling me Angel then it dawned on me. "My stage name!"

In the natural daylight, Deedee's thought to be bleach blonde hair was a light blonde with highlights, her before straight tresses were now loose curls that dropped inches below her recently modified set of "D" cup breasts that only the best plastic surgeon in town could have provided. Her 120 lb frame was laid out like a pencil drawn figure highlighting all the right places of her body. She was barely 5'5" without her six-inch heels. Her light brown eyes were a perfect contrast to her olive skin, which was made even darker from the combination of the Florida sun and her Latino bloodline.

"I'm sorry," she said, "I couldn't remember your name."

"It's Samantha," I replied. Smiling Deedee said, "I never told you my real name. It's Dianna. Deedee is my stage name." "What happened? I haven't seen you at work." "Oh, I've been thinking about stuff," I said. People were starting to tune in to our conversation, so I decided to change the subject.

"Do you live around here?" I asked her. "Oh, no, I'm waiting for my lawyer," she said. She must have read the confusion on my face. Then she said, "It's a long story. You'd have to sit for this one." After getting my food, Deedee signaled me to join her at her table and without hesitation she said, "I'm going through a divorce, can you believe I was married for three years, to this asshole name Louis. Anyway, my lawyer's office is right down the street and she's supposed to swing by on her way to the airport to drop me some papers. She was biting into her sandwich when a short middle-aged woman approached our table. "Hello, Mrs. Sanchez," she said with her mouth full as the women reached our table. "Hello, Dianna," she replied in a much deeper voice than one would expect then turned to acknowledged my presence with a casual greeting. "I'm sort of in a rush but please read over the files and give me a call with whatever questions you might have. I won't be in until Friday so you'll have a few days to look them over." Deedee got up, as she took the yellow envelop from Mrs. Sanchez and walked her outside.

Minutes later, Deedee came back, with glossy eyes. I could tell she was holding back tears and that the smile on her face was forced. "Are you okay?" I asked her. "I have to be," she said. "It's been almost a year and I still can't deal with this shit." I was dying to know what the story was, but didn't want to intrude. As if reading my mind, Deedee started on the story of her life.

"I met Louis when I first got to the United States from Argentina. I didn't know anybody and Louis was ready to help. He was loaded with money from dealing drugs and whatever else he did. I was always attracted and fascinated by the macho bad boy kind of guy. Anyway I had to find a way to make a living but I didn't have papers to work in the country so Louis got me my first dancing job at a club owned by one of his clients. I don't even know how we started sleeping together but it wasn't like a serious relationship because Louis had one of those "good girl" kind of girlfriend in Hialeah that just worshiped the ground that he walked on. I was more like dessert for Louis because I'd allow him to be himself. I was the one he'd come to whenever he wanted to celebrate a deal, smoke a few joints, do a few lines or act out his sexual fantasies. It was common for us to go to a club, pick out a couple of nice-looking girls and take them home for the night. Well Louis' girlfriend somehow found out about us and she broke up the engagement thinking that he was gonna run back a changed man begging her to marry him but instead he came and proposed to me.

Soon after the wedding we started having problems; Louis kept bringing girls to our bed like before when we weren't married. I tried to talk to him about it but he had a fit. He said he didn't marry me so I could change him and that if he wanted a normal wife he would have married his ex-girlfriend. She paused a moment with a distant look in her eyes, then went on. "Then I found out that the asshole didn't want any kids, which at first was fine with me but then I unexpectedly got pregnant. When I told him, he got all piss off and accused me of trying to ruin his life.

That night I made my first trip to the emergency room with a broken nose, a black eye, a dislocated jaw and shoulder, then he made sure I got rid of the baby. Between my face and the loss of my baby I was a mess. Then before I could fully recover Louis ordered me back to work. It's like he was trying to punish me. With all the illegal money he had, he could have easily afforded to keep me home, but he kept telling me to take my ass back to work, and how he wasn't gonna support me while I was sitting on my ass at home doing shit.

After my recovery, I got involved in his business by making deliveries or running errands whenever needed. Working in a strip bar made it convenient for people to come by and pick up their merchandise from me without suspicion so Louis capitalized on that. Things seemed to be getting better but they were never the same. Louis was being nice again and we were more like roommates or business partners with special privileges. Our lives had turned into a rotation between getting high, getting drunk, having sex and sometimes work in between. We partied hard but when things went wrong, I'd pay the price dearly with bruises and broken bones. The sad thing was I was so fucked up most of the time that I was willing to stay and put up with it.

One night I was suppose to go to work and decided to go back home because I wasn't feeling very good and found Louis in bed with one of the girls that I used to work with. I just lost it, I picked up the iron that was lying on the bedroom floor and threw it at him before launching at the bitch on my fucking bed. The iron caught him on the side of his head leaving him in need of ten stitches and me, a busted jaw and a cracked rib. It had only been a little bit over a year but by then, I knew I had to leave him, I just couldn't take it anymore.

When I got back from the hospital, I made the mistake of asking him for a divorce, and from then on my life has been a living hell. He never gave me an answer, but it was obvious that he didn't want a divorce. We were going through the process for getting my green card so he told me he was gonna get me deported if I tried to leave him, but at this point I didn't really care. We were barely talking although we lived in the same house and whenever possible I'd wait for him to go to sleep so I could crash on the couch or in the spare room. Months went by and in my mind we were through, I was just buying time to save enough money to get my own place and get out of this mess.

Then I met Ashley at the gym and for the first time, I had someone I could talk to about my problems and take my mind off of things. We were not planning on it but somehow got closer than we intended and one afternoon Louis came home unexpectedly and caught us in bed. He was supposed to be out of town and nearly killed me after chasing Ashley out of the house. I begged and pleaded for him to give me a divorce but I doubt he heard me through all his yelling. When he was done with me he told me to take my ass to work because one of his buyers was coming for a pick up, I had bruises all over my body and didn't know how he expected me to go to work but he just kicked me out saying that he didn't want to deal with me tonight. On my way to work, I got pulled over by these two cops who mysteriously wanted to search my car. They found two bags of cocaine that Louis' customer was supposed to come by the club for in my bag. I pleaded and tried to tell them that it wasn't mine but they wouldn't listen. Next thing I knew, there were five police cars around me and I was being handcuffed, read my rights, and dragged off to jail. Deep down I just knew that Louis had something to do with it.

I was charged with drug trafficking and Louis wouldn't even come to bail me out. I called Nick, one of my customers, and he thankfully bailed me out. I then found out that Louis was having me followed, which is how he found out about my relationship with Ashley and purposely set me up. It's not like Louis and I had anything going on anyway. All this drama just because I busted his ego.

When I went to court he testified against me claiming that I was an unfit wife, a drug addict, a bi-sexual whore and a stripper. With a jury of mostly conservative middle-aged women I never had a chance. I spent two months in jail and thank goodness with Nick's connection I was able to get out on probation."

You could tell Deedee was extremely upset and she had good reason to be. She stayed quiet for a while, fighting back her emotions. Then out of the blue, she asked me what my plans were for the night. I had to go find a cheap motel for the night, but I was willing to trade that for some company. "Nothing important," I answered. "Well, I have a party to go to tonight. Would you like to come?" I was thinking of the kind of party that someone with stories like

Deedee would be having when she added with a reassuring voice. "It's a birthday celebration party for my boyfriend, I got him a couple of girls to pop out of a birthday cake but don't worry, nothing weird. Nick is nothing like Louis, he doesn't have that kind of appetite. You should come; it's gonna be fun." I had to get ready and take a shower, and Deedee said I could get ready at her place. So I followed her home.

The drive was about 20 minutes from where we were. We reached her complex and went up her private elevator to the tenth floor. Deedee occupied a two bedroom, two-bath penthouse, with a balcony view of the bay. Each bedroom had access to a bathroom. The first room she took me to was her guest room occupied by a large bed dressed in Victorian style print pillows and comforter. A small desk on the left side of the bed held a Tiffany lamp and a small computer. Directly across from the bed was a TV stand supporting a 32" screen television. Pictures of Deedee and a few floral prints occupied the wall. Deedee's room was richly furnished. Her king-size wooden bed had a post in each corner reaching almost to the ceiling. Her dresser took up most of the left wall leading to the walk-in closet, which was a room in itself. A Persian rug lay in front of the bed and a knee high wooden chest rested against the end of the bed. A small room connecting to the bathroom was furnished with a copper princess high chair with a matching vanity table. That was covered with makeup, perfume, and a few pieces of jewelry. An exotic plant on a stand stood next to the bathroom door. We went through the bathroom, where I noticed the ivory hot tub, then back into the impressively large and furnished living room. "How long have you been living here?" I asked her. "Almost a year," she said, "right after I got out of jail. Nick and I started dating, I didn't wanna go back home to Louis so Nick pulled a few strings, got me this place and helps me out with the bills. Believe me, I could never afford this place and most of these things on my own."

We took Deedee's 1992 BMW and drove for an hour to get to North Miami Beach for the party. As we drove, Deedee told me stories about her married life, her present relationship, stories about the girls at the club, and stupid jokes about the customers. With her talking, the ride didn't seem as long as it really was. The music from the party could be heard from outside as we approached the two story house. A girl wearing barely anything opened the door and gave me a puzzled look. When she spotted Deedee behind me, her attitude suddenly changed and she happily told us to come in. Deedee showed me around, introduced me to some of the people that she knew, and then she went around looking for her boyfriend. We found Nick on his downstairs patio with three guys smoking fat Cuban cigars. Deedee went around kissing the guys on the cheek and laid a fat juicy kiss on the olive skinned black hair man, whom I assumed, was Nick. Nick, like the other men standing around, couldn't have been any more than 5'10" or 5'11". He had a little bit of a belly indicating that he had no problem with food, but his physique clearly stated that he was no couch potato. I said hello and stood still waiting for Deedee. When they were done with their kiss, Deedee introduced me to every one of the guys and told them I was a friend of hers from work. "Come on," she said once that was done "let's go get something to drink, anybody else want anything?" She turned around and asked the guys." "We're all good mama, just hurry back with your fine ass," said Nick as he blew rings of smoke towards her.

We tried to make our way to the bar but with everybody coming up and talking to Deedee, we never had a chance to get our drinks. One of the guys from outside came in and told Deedee that the girls for the pop up cake were ready to go and Nick was already upstairs waiting for her. She asked me if I wanted to go upstairs with her and watch the girls but the DJ was playing some good tunes and watching two girls take off their clothes for a bunch of horny man did not appeal to me so I told her I was gonna stay downstairs and have a bit of fun for a change. Deedee vanished up the stairs as I made my way to an empty stool at the bar. "Club soda please," I requested and as I waited for my drink, the smell of cigarette, cigar and especially marijuana filled the air. The ventilation for this house was clearly not intended for this kind of event. A man with two girls sharing a joint approached the bar; he called out for three beers. He looked over pointing the joint toward me and said, "Wanna join the party?" "No thanks," I replied. The two girls giggled, grabbed their beer and dragged him away. I was finishing my drink waiting for a good song to dance to, when this man came and asked me to dance with him. He was tall and dark with nice long dreads. I was about to say no, and then looking at his gorgeous face, I decided to give it a go. Some good selections were being played when we reached the dance floor, and boy, could he dance! My shirt was soaked with sweat by the time his friends came by and told him they were leaving. I was making my way back to the bar for a beer, when one of the guys from the patio came up to asked me to dance. "You probably don't remember my name but "I'm Tim." I'd heard so many names that night that he was correct about me not remembering his name but, I didn't want to be rude so I said, "Hey Tim, I'm…" He interrupted and said "Angel?" He sounded so excited as if he was gonna get a prize for remembering my name. "Yeah" I said with a smile "I guess you remembered."

With my heels on, Tim was barely a couple of inches taller than me. The next few hours that followed we went back and forth between the bar and the dance floor. Being in an unfamiliar setting I stopped my alcohol intake after my third beer just in case something happened and I needed to get out of there; after all, I didn't know Deedee that well. I was probably the only sober person at that party and I was actually having a good time.

I didn't know what time it was, but I was getting tired and thought I should look for Deedee and find out when we were leaving. I made my way upstairs, there was a glass door leading to a terrace with outdoor furniture occupied by people drinking and smoking. Deedee was sitting on Nick's lap, talking to this couple. They were sharing a joint and giggling. As much as I wanted to know when we were leaving at the moment it no longer seemed that important.

Not wanting to disturb them, I made my way back to the bar and got a cold glass of water. People were starting to leave and some of the couches in the living room were now empty. I went into the living room and sat back in a comfortable chair. The dance floor in the front room was deserted, a few people were passed out on the couches, and others were making out in various places around the room. I started to feel sleep creeping up on me. When I finally spotted a clock it was 3:45 A.M. and Deedee was finally making her way down the stairs. It was obvious she was having a hard time carrying her drink, let alone walking. I walked towards her, seeing that she was definitely wasted. There's no way I was going to let this girl drive us back. I didn't have a death wish tonight. "Are we leaving?" I asked her casually. "Yup, aszz soon as I find my keyssz," she said, waddling around in front of me. I took the glass from her and walked her to a chair. I asked her for her bag, which I assumed would have her keys. I went up to the balcony to look. A girl was busy going down on some guy and an older guy was asleep on one of the lounge chairs. I spotted the bag under one of the tables, grabbed it and made my way back downstairs. Nick was standing next to Deedee, just as wasted, talking about us staying for the night. Although I didn't have a place to stay I really didn't feel comfortable spending the night there. I told him I didn't mind driving and thank goodness they didn't make a fuss about it.

Deedee was really freaking me out on the way home; one minute she was laughing and the next she would start crying. She was telling me all kinds of stories about her life and her childhood. By the time we made it back to her place, I knew more than I needed to know about her. Getting her to the elevator was a task in itself. As soon as we made it inside she ran to the bathroom and for the few minutes that followed, all you could hear was Deedee barfing her guts out. I wanted to go in and help but I barely knew the girl and I had no experience in handling these matters. I called her name a few times just to see if or what I could do but she never answered. Reluctantly, I approached the bathroom door and heard the shower running. I knocked and waited then finally she answered and said she'd be okay. I went back to the living room uncertain about what I should do. I was exhausted and I didn't even know where I was going to sleep yet. Shortly after, Deedee came into the living room. She was in her bath robe with a towel wrapped around her head. "I'm sorry," she said, "I hope I didn't scare you?" As she talked I stood and stared at her trying to figure out how she went from being wasted to whatever she was at the moment. "Are you okay?" I asked her. "Yes, I'll be fine, I just had a little too much fun." She headed for the kitchen and asked me if I wanted a cup of coffee. I was really tired so I thought the coffee would do good and hopefully wake me up since I still had to go find myself a room for the night.

It was 12:15 P.M. when I woke up and realized I was lying on Deedee's couch. I must have fallen asleep when she went to get the coffee. I got up feeling a little out of place. I was thinking to myself, I just met the girl and here I was in her living room smelling like sweat and cigarettes thanks to last night's party. At that moment Deedee came in holding towels and a set of clothes.

"Hey girl, I'm sorry I didn't wake you up but you looked like you needed the rest. I hope I didn't mess up your schedule." "No," I answered, "I didn't have anything to do, I just didn't want to impose." "Oh please!" she said, "It's not like I don't have enough room, besides I didn't know how I was going to get home if it wasn't for you. Oh! Before I forget do you want me to call you Angel or Samantha?" "Samantha, if you don't mind." "All right mama, I have towels in the bathroom, cereal, milk and bagels in the kitchen so help yourself." As I headed for her kitchen she made her way to her couch, turned on the large screen TV and yelled. "Tim called this morning, seemed like you guys had a good time." I don't know if she was waiting for some details from me but there was none so I just confirmed her statement that I did have a good time. When I joined her in the living room after my shower with my bagel and coffee she asked me if I was going to work that night and I found myself saying yes. With no intention in making sense out of my decision, the fact was I needed this job. She had some running around to do for the day and proposed that I go with her since I didn't have much to do.

The day went by and I hardly had time to think of my situation. I had a blast with Deedee. She was an absolute riot. One had to try really hard to not have a good time with this girl. By the end of the day it seemed as if we'd known each other forever and the first time since my father's death, I found myself talking about recent trials of my life.

By 8:00 P.M. Deedee and I were at the Unicorn Lounge in the dressing room. My heart was pounding so loud that I could swear that everyone could hear it. That night and every other night that followed seemed a tortuous experience which like my first night at the Unicorn was filed somewhere in the back of my mind. Starting my night with a Long Island Ice Tea and two shots of Tequila gradually became a ritual and many a night I would leave work not knowing how much money I made or how I got to my car.

My first day back at the club, Deedee offered me her guest room until I could find a place to stay. My other option was a motel room and though I didn't know Deedee for long, I decided to take up her offer.

The difference between Dianna at home and Deedee at the club was night and day. At the club she was not the easy-going, nor the friendly type. Most of the girls were jealous of her, yet respected her. She was probably the club's top girl, in terms of making money. Although she didn't and wouldn't do some of the things that a lot of the other girls did, she had a solid line of customers who kept her busy with private dances, bottles of champagne and occasional drug deals. She talked to everyone at the club but it was obvious that her relationship with the girls was as Deedee not Dianna. How I ended up in Dianna's world is beyond me. She could have easily let me be as everyone else had done but for whatever reason she crossed my path when I needed a friend and she has and will always be.

Dianna took me under her wing at the club. Her customers became mine and the few that I made we also shared. We worked the same schedule; carpooled and by the end of our nights we'd joke about who would have the biggest hang over the next day. Of course, it would always be me considering she was a veteran in the field. Weeks went by and I still couldn't find a place. Hurricane Andrew made it hard to find any vacancies. I really felt as if I was imposing on Dianna's kindness but she would have none of that. Whenever I'd bring the topic up she'd say, "I remember what I went through when I first got here from Argentina. I was in the streets with nowhere to go and if it wasn't for Louis I don't know what I would have done. I guess that is why I still feel some sort of gratitude towards him no matter how much I hate him for what he's done to me. These streets are no place for anyone to be…" she was quiet for a while then she went on. "I'm not doing this so you could feel obligated to me, think of it as a favor to me." Dianna was talking as if she was way older than me but at 25 years of age she had had more than her share of heartache. Although Nick covered most of the expenses of the apartment, Dianna eventually agreed on splitting the utility bills.

Christmas rolled up and both Deedee and I were not in the mood to cele-brate. She was going through some court hearing regarding her divorce and I was missing my father immensely. We worked all day and night just to keep ourselves occupied but with everyone being so jolly it was kind of hard to escape the "noel" sensation.

CHAPTER 6

It was June, a Wednesday afternoon eight months from the day I started dancing. I was working a split shift, meaning half of the day shift and half of the night shift from 4:00 P.M. to 12:00 A.M. While Deedee was away visiting with Nick it was about 6:30 P.M. and business was somewhat slow. The few customers that we had were being hustled by the daygirls who were coming towards the end of their shift at 8:00 P.M. I had about $80.00 in my boots and about six more hours to go, so I knew I had time to make some real money by the end of the night. I was sitting in the back end of the bar watching Karen make conversation with the few customers at the bar when this guy walked in. Though I didn't make a point in noticing every customer that walked through the Unicorn Lounge door, this man caught my attention. His attire reminded me of a rain forest tour guide with that Sean Connery kind of look. He couldn't have been more than 60 years old but had a full head of white hair with matching facial hair. The look he carried portrayed intelligence and class, among other things. He made his way to one of the back tables. Karen told the waitress walking by the bar that Stanley was here, as she pointed at the white haired man. As Karen handed the waitress a bottle of Perrier, I asked her if Stanley was a regular. "Don't bother," she answered me. "This guy holds on to his money."

I smiled at her comment as I headed for the stage. The DJ played "My Name is not Susan," by Whitney Houston, and "I want your sex" by George Michael. And throughout my performance Stanley kept looking at me. It wasn't one of those usual looks that came from the customers; it was as if he was studying me. I soon got off the stage to make my rounds. When I got to him, he placed a couple of dollars in my garter and said "Nice show." "Thank you," I said, and fixed the bills around my garter belt. "Are you a dancer?" he asked me with an

English accent. For a moment I was thinking, this man must be really stupid to be asking me if I was a dancer, where did he think he was, at the library? He must of have seen my awkward look.

"I'm sorry," he said. "What I meant was are you a performer like ballet, Jazz, etc?" "I used to be," I said, and paused for a minute. This last comment brought back memories of me being in school, so I left it at that then moved on.

I completed my rounds and headed back to the bar and the feeling of being watched was upon me as I took my previous seat. I looked around and noticed Stanley looking my way. He'd been there a while, yet none of the girls were attempting to even get close to him. I thought back on the warnings made by Karen, but what did I have to lose? There were hardly any customers and I was not in the mood to hustle so maybe I can get an intelligent conversation out of him. With no expectation of making money, I headed toward Stanley.

"Mind if I join you?" I asked. "Not if you don't mind breaking the curse," he answered. "The curse?" I asked, while several different thoughts popped into my head. "Yes" he said with a smirk. "The girls have known for a while that I don't have time for the whole charade of buying drinks, private dances and such, so they stay clear of me." I was in no mood for games, so going back to my stool would have been just as good. I asked him if that was a warning for me to go away. But he kindly pulled out the chair next to him and invited me to sit.

As I anticipated, he was well worth talking to. Stanley Wellington was an Englishman and a widower of fifteen years with two grown sons. Apart for the brief explanation about his children, he did not talk much about himself nor his family. We ventured more towards general yet, worthwhile topics. Then, we found our plateau at law and psychology.

An hour passed quickly, and it was my time to go back on stage. Stanley asked me to come back if I had a chance and I eagerly agreed to return. My performance lasted a brief 7 minutes. As I headed towards the customers near the bar to collect my contributions, Karen signaled for me to come to her. "How did you get him to order that bottle?" she asked. I didn't quite know what she was talking about, but I let her go on. "Do you know how long it's been since Stanley has spent money on any girl in here? You want it half and half?

Half and half is the term when the dancer wants the bartender to mix some of her drinks with apple cider. The bartender would take a glass from the bottle sup-posedly for herself, she would then go to the bar empty the glass to replace it with apple cider then bring the glass back to the table switching it with the dancer's portion without the customer noticing. This process can go on for the entire bottle depending on the girl's request. Of course the commission made from the bottle would be shared with the bartender.

I answered yes to Karen's question and looked back to see the tall bottle of Moet in front of Stanley. For the first time since I started dancing, I actually felt bad for a customer spending unnecessary money. Stanley was the first customer since I started dancing who had treated me like a human being rather than some fantasizing sex object. Perhaps his smaller head was no longer in action, which prevented him from being stupid, but somehow I doubted Stanley was ever in that category. I headed toward my overpriced chilled bottle and Stanley welcomed me with a smile. We started right where we left off our conversation that went on for a few hours. Around 10:30 P.M. Stanley left, promising to come back and see me.

When I walked in Deedee's place, I found her crying on the floor with a split lip and some apparent bruises on her arm. I dropped my bag and rushed to the floor near her. "What happened?" I asked her with panic in my voice. She kept crying for a moment then blurted, "Louis is what happened." I rubbed her shoulder not knowing what to do but she kept on crying. I wasn't sure what she meant and wondered if it was a good time for questions, but then she went on. "I came home and found Louis and my parole officer outside waiting for me. He claimed that I've missed two court appearances and failed to sign up for counseling and rehab so now I'm back in court and this time he said they might lock me up for good."

I am still confused since that didn't explain how she got all these bruises.

She cried some more then went on in between sobs, "I followed Louis home to find out what the heck was going on, we got into this big fight and that's when that happened" pointing to her lip.

I was still puzzled, things just didn't add up. It's well known that some people didn't believe in divorce but how sick is this Louis guy to be taking it so far, after all it's not like they were still together. What is he to gain by making Deedee's life miserable? Certainly not love. I was in deep thought when Deedee started talking in her sobbing voice again. "I sent him the divorce papers four month's ago and he sent them back all torn up in the envelope. I just want to move on with my life you know," she paused, "anyway I was kind of pissed off then, I found out that he had a deal lined up, a drug deal," she looked at me as if to make sure I followed, "Well, I knew some of the guys involved, and one of the guys wanted to get back at Louis because he fucked him over a couple of times. The guy was leaving the country anyway, so I helped him."

This was clearly a pissing contest between two hardheaded people and in the process they were just hurting themselves. I wanted to ask Deedee what she meant by helping the guy and how Louis found out, but this was heading somewhere I didn't want to go, therefore, the less I knew the better.

The next few days that followed Nick and Deedee were in and out of the County Court Room, making sure that she didn't go to jail. By the end of the week, Deedee was on probation and was ordered to sign up for rehab. One would think that would be the end of it but she was already planning on how she was gonna get back at Louis.

Stanley would stop by the club once or twice a week just to say hello. The concept of taking or expecting money could never click in my mind, so slowly I was starting to see him as a friend. He never asked me for private dances and would often surprise me with a few hundreds during his visits but strangely enough he would never put them in my garter belt. He would place them in between a napkin or, on occasions in books, which he'd bring for me to read. As I learned a little more about Stanley, I told him about my previous years at the University, and from then on he would constantly remind me of how I needed to get back in school, and stop wasting my talents in this business. One Thursday night, Stanley came to see me at work. I was busy with table dances and such so it took me a while to get to him. Some of the girls made their way to his table but shortly left him with a look of defeat on their faces. To this I found a string of satisfaction. I made it to the dressing room where Deedee, who had been drinking like a fish, was asleep on the counter. I checked and made sure her money was deep down her thigh high boots and left the room making a mental note to come back and wake her before her turn on stage. I made my way to Stanley and twice was stopped by customers requesting private table dances. I told them I'd return and found Stanley all dressed up in a black suit waiting for me. The suit made him look a lot younger than his sixty some years old. "Got a hot date?" I teased him.

"No," he said, "I had a court hearing today." Stanley was a well-established lawyer. He volunteered this information to me not too long ago. The law firm had been in his family now for three generations. His father started it back in England and slowly made their way into the States. His brother still runs the branch in England and Stanley and his two sons, run the ones in the States. I remember him mentioning one in New York, Chicago and Miami. If there were others, I can't say I remember. With enough associates, there was no need for Stanley to work but I don't think he'd know what to do with himself if he stopped practicing law.

"Are you still looking for a place?" he asked. "Yes, do you have something for me?" I asked. I'd mentioned my search for a place to Stanley sometime last week, while talking about Hurricane Andrew and the mess it left behind. "I made a few calls and I think I might have something for you, so if you're interested you can go look at it and let me know." said Stanley. "Where is it located?" I asked him. "Not too far from the University of Miami," he said these words as he placed the address and direction of the place on the table along with a calendar from the university with the schedule for the upcoming term. "I took the liberty of bringing you the schedule for the next term, just in case you thought about going back to school, hope you don't mind." "No Stanley, I don't mind," I replied with a smile and gratefully gave him a hug. For the first time it dawned on me why I felt so relaxed, and secure around Stanley. He was like a father figure to me. Whether he was talking about my not being in school, my job or self-destructive drinking habits, he always knew how to do it in such a way that I'd always know he wasn't trying to impose.

Stanley left shortly after, and I resumed with my job. The idea of the possibility of me finally finding a place was exciting. I rushed to the dressing room to tell Deedee about the news but she didn't seem as excited as I was. "I'm hardly gonna to see you now," she said sadly. "Come on," I said, "you should know me better than that; me moving should have no bearing on our friendship." "You're right," she said with a forced smile on her face. I pulled her off the stool and told her that she was next to go on stage. She freshened up a bit and out the door we went. As the night progressed, Deedee got closer to her usual cheery self. And with me being all excited, it made a perfect match for a moneymaking night.

A few days later I went to see the place and met with Stanley. The building was an out-of-the-way six unit's timeshare golf club complex. The unit that Stanley spoke to me about was a luxurious one bedroom, one bath, dining room/kitchen combo, a living room extended with a half pie shaped balcony overlooking the green. It was cozy and absolutely beautiful so when he told me that his client wanted $600.00 a month for the place, I did not hesitate to accept the deal. The place was minutes away from University of Miami and close to the few shops that were reopening including some major malls. In this market, this place could have been rented for a lot more so I'm sure Stanley had something to do with my getting this deal.

July 1994 had just rolled up and it seemed like things were finally going to be okay. I now had my own place, getting back in school was two months away, the club anniversary party which was a for sure easy money night was coming up and I was two weeks away from my 21st birthday.

CHAPTER 7

The club's anniversary party was schedule to start at 7:00 P.M. on Friday July 14th. By 6:00 P.M. the parking lot was half full with cars. With all the advertisements running in the radios and local newspapers, a big turnout was expected. It was the only time the customers had a chance to get something from the club. A buffet table was overloaded with bar food and all the beers a customer could handle was on the house from seven until midnight.

The dancers were all prettied up with their wigs, make-up, and new outfits. Deedee and I had two outfits for the night; one being matching leather short set, with matching bustier, one black for Deedee and a white one for me. Anniversary Night was a big deal at the club. Girls have bragged about going home with two grand from the event. This was my first and I had every intention on breaking that two grand record.

When Deedee joined me at the bar for our usual kick-start of Tequila shots, customers could be seen from every corner of the place. With 42 girls on the floor, our performances were reduced to a one song set instead of the usual two. Table dances were in every corner, and girls were on and off of them continuously. Right after my first stage performance, Deedee called me into the Champagne Room for a private dance for one of her customers. He (the customer) was already seated ready for his treat. Deedee and I got on the narrow table and started our performance. Having danced together so many times, we now had a few routines worked out to perfection "from schoolgirls to dominatrix." With matching outfits, we started our twin routine. Deedee slowly took off my boostier, and then turned around so I'd do the same for her. We danced topless watching the customer enjoying the two pairs of boobs only inches away from him. I then moved behind Deedee, pulled her hair up as she played with her D-cup breasts. My hands let go of her hair, moved down her waist and snapped the side buttons of her shorts, then pulled them through her slightly open legs. Then her hands now reached behind for my hips, with one hand I again picked up her hair leaving some strands hanging and my other hand helping her undo my shorts as previously done to her. The customer smiled as Deedee turned to face me acting as if she was going down on me. The song ended, the customer signaled us to keep on and so we did. With one finger in my mouth, my other hand rested on Deedee's hair who was slowly coming back up to join me on the small table. We danced a total of four songs, then the guy placed a one hundred dollar bill in each of our garters. I was called to go on stage so, I rushed up to the beat of "I Promise" by When In Rome and left Deedee with the customer.

Towards the end of the final seconds of my performance, a group of about five guys all suited up, walked through the door. From afar, they had the look of overdressed, underpaid office men. The last one had his tie loosened and his hair wild as if it had been playing in the wind. They were making their way towards the back and as they passed the bar, the last one stopped to catch my last moves.

As I went around the brass pole, I caught a glimpse of his face. He was gorgeous. He made his way through the crowd to the front of the bar, as I got off the stage.

The next girl was going up for her performance and I was snapping my clothes back on, when I heard the voice from behind. "Can I help you with that?" Common question asked by customers, so whoever it was would get my usual response. Without turning to see the origin of the voice I answered, "No thanks, I think I can manage." "I'm sorry I missed your show," the voice said, "are you available for a private dance?"

I turned around and there stood the guy with the loosened tie. Even with his hair all messed up he looked good. He placed a $20.00 in between my breast with a smile on his face as he waited for my answer to his question. I had a few dances lined up so I told him that as soon as I was done I would be available for his dance. He made his way to the back to join his friends as I went around for my contributions.

With so much money to be made, I didn't have time to waste, I took five minutes in the dressing room to freshen up and I was back on the floor. The DJ had just announced a 3 for 2 special, meaning for the next hour the private dances would be three dances for the price of two.

Between the private dances and the drinks that I had lined up, I totally forgot about the guy with the loosened tie until one of the bartenders came by and told me that a customer in the back wanted to know when I would be ready for his private dances. "Tell him I'll be there as soon as I can," "Make it fast," she whispered. "He's loaded."

The bartender left and I hopped on the stool in front of the customer who'd been patiently waiting for me. I was on song number 5 when Kevin, one of the managers, walked in the private booth informing me that I was needed in the back and that the customer had been waiting for a while meaning I had to put my other customers on hold to go cater to this guy. I knew exactly whom he was referring to, and the whole concept of this guy sending a manager to get me pissed me off. (*Whenever you have managers and bartenders catering to a customer with special care especially on a night as such, you know the customer's pocket is very deep, someone big or, usually both.*)

I excused myself to the guy I was dancing for and made my way to the back. About six or eight girls were sitting with the five guys in the suits among which, Mr. Hair in the Wind was being taken care of by two girls. I took a seat on the coffee table in front of him and said "I'm not available to dance for you, so please stop sending people to get me, besides, it seems like you're being taken care of, pointing to the two girls on either side of him then walked off.

2:00 A.M. and $2,800.00 later, the day shift girls were gone along with most of the customers, since the free drinks were over. Halfway sober, I was sitting at the bar with Deedee waiting for my turn to go on stage when I felt someone approaching. I turned to look and it was the guy that I never got to dance for. He bent down to kiss Deedee on the cheek and told her that he was leaving. "Already?" she asked. "Yeah, I'm going fishing with your old man tomorrow morning, got to get some sleep." Then he turned to me and said, "It doesn't look like I'm gonna get a dance from you tonight so I'll take a rain check. Here's my card maybe you can give me a call sometime." I smiled and took the card from him, which read "Danny R. Shapiro/Cargo Express..." something about import and exporting in South America and the Caribbean.

As the five of them exited the club, I turned to Deedee and asked her how she knew this guy. She told me that he was an old buddy of Nick's and that sometimes they did business together. Nick owned a car transportation company but most of his money came from drug transactions. I wasn't sure which of the two lines of business that Danny was sometimes involved in with Nick but I was willing to bet the latter.

Saturday, July 29th, the day of my 21st birthday, Deedee and Stanley planned to take me out for breakfast. Deedee stayed over from the night before so by 8:00 A.M. Stanley picked us up and headed to some overpriced cafe in the Gables. For the first time in a long time I felt really happy. I was with the only two friends I had in the world, thinking of the changes that were necessary in my life, and I was actually looking forward to making them. I knew I had to get back in school, stop or at least cut down on the drinking, and figure out a way to get out of dancing, among many other things. After breakfast we headed for Stanley's yacht where his two sons and a two of their friends, Jeremy and Donald, were waiting for us with balloons and Happy Birthday banners. Deedee, who was apparently in on it, wasn't surprised. I was speechless. I couldn't believe they went through so much trouble for my birthday.

Stanley's sons, Andrew and Anthony, were quite charming. Andrew, the oldest one was without a doubt a ladies man. His clean-cut light brown hair danced with the blowing wind. His green eyes sported a devious look that could only be found in a dirty magazine. He was also very carefree and outgoing. Anthony, on the other hand, seemed more like his father; reserved, yet friendly. He looked very much like his older brother except he had brown eyes and the blonde hair. It was close to noon when we finally settled in. Jeremy and Andrew were navigating the boat, Deedee was at the bar playing cards with Donald and Anthony, and I was on deck with Stanley listening to his offer for a part-time job at his firm. Apparently one of their secretaries moved and they needed someone part-time at least for a couple of days a week to help with the paper work. I knew it'd be good for me and would get me thinking about becoming a lawyer again but I didn't know if I could and if I was willing to do that. It was the first time that I realized how much I was hooked to this new lifestyle of big money, big spending, drinking and partying. The urgency of finding a job had taken a back seat in my mind. Stanley told me that I didn't have to give him an answer right away but I knew if I didn't I'd find a excuse to not do it so I told him I'd take the job.

I stayed on the chair while Stanley went down to the bar to get us something to drink and for some reason I felt like I was being watched. I turned around and spotted Anthony with Andrew behind the ship's wheel, Andrew was pointing to something in the water while Anthony was looking over my way. When our eyes met we both smiled, he raised his beer acknowledging that he was looking at me and turned to his brother. That was the third time I caught him looking at me. I turned around wondering why my heart kept skipping a beat every time Anthony looked my way. I closed my eyes and reared my thoughts to more practical issues such as how I could cut down my days at the club and work at the firm on Mondays and Wednesdays.

We were having so much fun that by 5:00 P.M., I was ready to crash. After a nice lunch, everyone was sitting on deck with their fishing lines waiting for a catch and I decided to go lay on the couch for a minute of rest. I was cleaning up the mess that was left in the living room from our early snack when Anthony appeared in the doorway. "Need any help?" he asked, as he sat on the opposite couch that was being cleaned. "No, not really. You guys have spoiled me enough for one day," I replied. My heart was starting to race but I tried to stay calm besides it was silly of me to have the heart for Stanley's son. "My father talks so much about you, it's nice to finally meet you," Anthony said with a lazy smile that revealed his dimples.

With everything put away, I got on the couch and listened to Anthony's stories about his dad, their work and his brother. Sitting across from him I had to admit he was easy on the eyes. The way his white cotton shirt laid on his body indicated that every inch of it was perfectly cut and defined. His out of place dirty blonde hair complemented his deep brown eyes and his lips wore this seductive smile that would make some women dream of being kissed by them. As I listened, I kept thinking of things I wish I could ask him. Things like if he had a girlfriend, if we could go out sometimes, if his lips felt as good as they looked. But there was no point in making a fool out of myself. I was so caught up between my thoughts and his voice that it took me a while to realize that he was referring to me as Samantha instead of my stage name Angel. I wondered if they knew about my job.

The day went by and as we headed back to port, we had cake and wine to finish the day. As we anchored the boat, Stanley made the announcement about my part-time job at the firm, and then the guys made Deedee promise to come by their office and visit. After my many thank-you's, it was time to go home. With only three cars, some arrangements had to be made for everybody to get home. Donald and Jeremy volunteered to take Deedee home. Donald had been eyeing Deedee since this morning and she sure didn't seem to mind so I wasn't surprise when she eagerly accepted. Stanley was exhausted from the long day and Andrew living the closest to him would take him home which left me with Anthony.

Anthony made me laugh the whole way home. As we played the question game, it was obvious that he didn't know about my job, and for some reason I was relieved. We talked about law school, college, his childhood, Stanley, etc. I had to be careful not to mention how Stanley and I met and thank God that it never came up. By the time we reached my place, I was wishing he didn't have to go; it was so easy to talk to him. Anthony had to help me bring my presents up and after offering him something to drink, we soon found ourselves watching old episodes of "The Three Stooges" until way past midnight. When the tapes finally ran out I was actually sad to see him go. We exchanged numbers and after a long birthday hug he disappeared behind the door.

This could easily be classified as one of the best days of my life. I wanted to call Deedee but I wasn't sure whether she had company or not, so with my father being a page away, I pulled my flower booklet and told him about my twenty-first birthday as I rewound one of the tapes and drifted to sleep watching "Three Stooges" once more.

CHAPTER 8

Sunday night Stanley called me to see if I wanted to come by the office tomorrow so he could introduce me to everybody since he was leaving for England that Wednesday. I eagerly said yes at the thought of seeing Anthony one more time. Once I got off the phone with Stanley I called Deedee to let her know that I wouldn't be going to work the next day since we usually car pooled. She was a little sad but happy for me. She told me about Saturday night how her and Donald went out drinking and didn't get home until 3:00 in the morning. "I hope you didn't do anything stupid," I said. But she nonchalantly said that they only played around and kissed. Leave it to Deedee. "What about Nick?" I asked. "What about Nick?" she repeated, "I'm just having fun girl, besides what Nick doesn't know won't hurt him." "You're such a whore," I teased her. She laughed and said, "I know."

10:00 A.M. Monday morning I reported to Stanley's firm "Wellington and Associates" near Coconut Grove. I gave the receptionist my name who immediately took me to see Stanley. Stanley's office was very traditional with dark wood and dark leather all over. Volume of books filled the shelves from floor to ceiling, awards, diplomas and pictures filled the back wall. There were a couple of framed pictures of him with his deceased wife and the boys in their younger days and of a more recent one of him and the boys. He smiled and told me to take a seat. Once the door was closed he told me what I would be doing and explained that under no circumstances was I to talk or mention anything about "Unicorn;" especially the fact that we met there. We went over some other minor details and then went around to be introduced to the crew. My heart was beating so fast and my hands were starting to sweat. I wanted to ask him if Anthony was here but didn't want him to know that I had a crush on his son. Stanley showed me where Andrew, Jeremy and Donald's offices were. The three were in the lobby when Stanley and I got upstairs. They all looked so different in their suits and ties. An older gentleman introduced as Dimitri McClain asked Stanley if he could borrow him for just a minute. Stanley excused himself and asked me to wait. As I waited, the boys came by to say hello and told me that I'd just missed Anthony who had a court hearing that morning. Donald asked me about Deedee and asked me to tell her to give him a call. They disappeared into their office and Stanley came out and finished the tour.

The building was three stories tall filled with lawyers of various ranks and fields of expertise. I left at 3:00 P.M. feeling as if I'd just completed hard physical labor. It's been so long since I had to use my mind in that capacity that I forgot how draining it could be.

That night Anthony called to say hi and see how my first day at the office was. I asked him about his hearing and before long we were on the phone for an hour talking about nothing relating to law.

Tuesday morning I woke up with Anthony on my mind. I thought about calling him but I didn't want to call him at work. The phone rang I picked it up hoping it would be him but it was Deedee calling to check on me. I told her about my first day at the office and she told me about the slow night she had. She barely made $100.00, which was unheard of for Deedee. I told her that Donald wanted her to give him a call. She laughed and said she'd think about it.

Around lunchtime, Anthony called. I was like a high school girl gleaming with happiness. He told me that he was leaving for lunch and wondered if I wanted to join him. Needless to say what my answer was. We met at a small café in Coconut Grove. Anthony was wearing black slacks with a white shirt and tie. He looked like a perfect picture cutout of a clothing magazine. We talked like old friends who hadn't seen each other in years. After lunch he walked me to my truck. I unlocked the door and as I turned around to say goodbye we found each other's lips for our first kiss. We stood there speechless by the emotion. I unconsciously got in the truck, rolled down the window without a word not wanting to break the spell or wake from my dream but it only got better. He pushed the door closed and found my lips through the open window. As we kissed, the unbearable humidity and the hot sun of South Florida disappeared, my heart stopped beating as his tongue explored the inside of my mouth. "Call me later" he said softly as he pulled his head out of the truck. I watched him walk to his car, still feeling the weight of his lips on mine. As I drove back home it dawned on me that I had to work tonight which meant I wouldn't be able to call Anthony.

I called him around 6:00 hoping to catch him before I left for work but then I remembered he'd still be at the gym. Deedee got to my place at 7:00 P.M. and I couldn't wait to tell her about me and Anthony. She was all excited and told me that I was finally starting to live life. Deedee was crazy so I didn't even wanna ask her what she meant by that. Before we left I called Anthony, left him a message, and told him that I was gonna be gone for the night and that I'd see him at the office the next day.

When I made it to work at the club, I was surprised by a vase of roses waiting for me in the office. It couldn't be Anthony since he didn't know about my job so it was probably one of my customers. The card read, "Still waiting for your call. Thinking of you! Danny."

I couldn't remember who Danny was, so I rushed to my locker, pulled out the shoebox packed with business cards and there it was "Danny R. Shapiro/ Cargo Express…" I put the flowers aside and proceeded to get ready for work. Deedee read the card from the flowers and immediately knew who they were from. "Now that's a man worth falling for," she said with a smirk on her face. "What's that suppose to mean?" I asked her defensively. "Think of all the excitement that can come with Danny, then think of Anthony. Not that I don't like him or anything but he's too proper, you need some excitement in your life," she exclaimed as she picked up her first shot of Tequila. I thought about saying the kind you have in your life? But I thought better of it because I know she doesn't mean anything by what she says I just wish she didn't talk about Anthony like that.

Wednesday went by like a blur at the office. Stanley left his secretary in charge of my training and apart from a quick hello, I never had a chance to talk to Anthony. When I walked to my truck that afternoon I spotted his car, I wrote him a note and stuck it under his wipers. The note read: *Missing you. Call me later.* And not wanting to sign Love you, *I wrote XOXO Samantha.* That night we talked for hours then fell asleep on the phone like two brainless teenagers.

The following week I was working at the club when Danny walked in as I was coming from the dressing room. He made his way to the bar and as he waited for his drink, I decided to go by and thank him for the flowers. He smiled, as I got near and pulled the stool next to him for me to sit. "Thanks for the flowers," I said. "I hope you liked them. Would you like something to drink?" I was feeling too normal and a shot or two was way overdue so I ordered a shot of Tequila. The bartender gave me this dirty look, because with the kind of money this guy had I should have been ordering Champagne but oh well.

It was a slow night and Danny insisted I sit with him for a while. He reproached me for not dancing for him and for ignoring him the last time he was in. According to him, his private dance was way overdue so we headed for the Champagne Room for my private performance. I got on the dance stool as "Smooth Operator" by Sade started to play. I was getting into my performance when he called my name and asked me to stop. No one has ever asked me to stop dancing before, so my mind was racing trying to figure out what was going on. I turned to face him waiting for an explanation. It looks like he was searching for the right words then he finally said in a slow and thoughtful tone. "You are so beautiful" he said, "I really came here to see you…I wanted to talk to you…I know you probably hear this all the time, but I would like to get to know you." "You're right," I said, "I do hear this all the time." I don't get paid for people to get to know me, and I don't date customers, so I guess I won't be able to help." I was about to get my outfit back on when he reached for my hand. "Fine," he said, "I would like as many dances as it would take for us to get to know each other" with that being said he pulled out three bills of $100 and placed them in my garter. I stood there for a second, amazed at his persistence. I got back on the dance stool and as the music played in the background, he started asking me the typical questions that customers always want to know. "How long have you been working at the club?" "Not long," I said, then thinking how I couldn't believe I'd been doing this for almost two years. "So you're a virgin at it hum?" he said with a corny smirk that revealed his perfectly lined teeth.

"Are we gonna dance or talk?" I asked him ignoring his corny comment. "I'm sorry" he said in a more serious tone "but I really want to get to know you. I don't know many girls that can make me nervous." "Maybe you should take it as a sign and move on." He ignored my comment and said "Deedee told me you guys are goooood friends." I could read the implication in his voice but I wasn't about to extend him the courtesy of a response. "Can you just let me dance?"

Eventually things did get better. No I never did "just dance." Danny wouldn't stop talking and asking questions but after awhile I didn't mind him so much. He even managed to make me laugh. I found out that he used to be a police officer, born and raised in the Florida Keys. He's a party animal, huge Dolphin's fan and had been friends with Nick and some of the other guys I met at Nick's birthday party since high school. He asked me if I had a boyfriend, where I was from, if I had any kids, etc…the only thing he got out of me was the yes on the boyfriend and no kids answer everything else relating to family history was off topic.

"Is Angel your real name?" he went on. "It will be for now," I answered. He was in the middle of his next question when I finally decided to take him up on his offer and sit down. Deedee came by to say hi to Danny so I seized the chance to ask her to join us. We sat in the Champagne Room, the bottles of Champagne kept coming, and pretty soon as the alcohol started kicking in we were laughing and talking as if we were enjoying each others company.

Without knowing, we started a weekly ritual with Danny. He would come in halfway through my shift and keep Deedee and me in the Champagne Room with him close to closing time. Sometimes he would bring a couple of guys with him, which I believed was intentionally done to keep Deedee company so he could talk to me privately. He would even have some of the other girls come in for private dances. Those nights were some of my best nights because although Danny rarely let me dance for him he made sure I was taken care of. I could always bet on a $300.00 to $400.00 nights whenever Danny came by and that didn't even include the commissions on the Champagne bottles. Sometimes I'd tease him and tell him that he'd be cheaper for him to get a shrink to talk to but his answer was that he had every intention of making me his girl sooner or later so therefore he didn't mind spending the money.

In the weeks that followed toward the end of August, I drove to the University of Miami and registered for the upcoming term. My Dodge pickup truck, which was way overdue for retirement, decided to break down on me. There were so many things wrong with this truck that it would take forever to get it back in top shape again. I knew that if it wasn't Daddy's old truck, I would have gotten rid of it a long time ago but enough was enough. It had liquid leaking all over the place, my gas gauge only worked when it wanted to, my transmission would not shift out of third gear and most importantly for South Florida, my air conditioning would only blow hot air. I had to find something reliable and with all the money I'd been saving it's not like I couldn't afford it. Deedee and I spent days cruising around shopping for a car. I called Stanley, who was still in England to get some advice and every other day he'd call to see what we'd found but with so many options I just couldn't make up my mind.

Two weeks from the day we started looking I found my car. A 1994 Black Mustang convertible fully loaded and since I was in the mood for shopping, I also got myself a cell phone. Deedee and I drove to Stanley's firm to show off my new ride and maybe do lunch with the boys. Stanley wasn't due back for another day or two but both Andrew and Anthony were there. After inspecting and congratulating me on my new car, we drove to Pizza Hut where Donald and Jeremy were waiting for us. Hanging with these guys was like being with a group of overgrown high school kids. One would never think these guys were young successful lawyers from the way they were behaving. An hour and a half later we were back in the parking lot at the office. Andrew had an appointment to run to and Jeremy had a meeting to attend. Anthony and Andrew were throwing a Retirement party for Stanley that Friday and insisted that we come. Stanley's retirement wasn't for another three months but he was only going to be in town for a couple of weeks before going back to England for three months so they were doing an early party. We were talking about the party while Donald and Deedee standing near by was flirting with each other. Watching the two of them got me all tongue twisted as I tried to keep the conversation going. Being in the parking lot of his work place Anthony and I didn't know how to act. Over the past weeks we were spending as much time together as our schedule would permit but with him being in a middle of a trial and my weird work schedules, it was kind of hard to set another "Three Stooges night." We started to walk as we talked about the hours he's put in this case then right before I got in my car he said "Sam…" I stopped to look at him wishing that I could kiss him but before he could even finish saying my name, Deedee approached the passenger door so he said he'd call me later. As we drove off he waved the invitation in the air as a reminder.

That night I didn't go to work just so I could talk to Anthony. Deedee was a little upset because Danny was supposed to come by. She told me that I was acting like a lovesick puppy in love but I didn't care. I'm not sure what being in love felt like but if that's what I was feeling, then it felt damn good. By 8:00 P.M. both Andrew and Anthony had already called seeing if I wanted them to pick Deedee and me up or if we were going to drive to the party ourselves. When I called Deedee at the club she told me I was on my own. Larry had asked her to work a private party that Friday and she couldn't say no. Deedee had told me about those private parties before and I know she didn't have much of a choice but to work them. Those private parties were held after hours for business transactions, celebration parties or any sort of business that could not be conducted in broad daylight. Only specific people were allowed to work them. Before I went to bed I called Anthony and told him I would take him up on his offer so I wouldn't have to drive to the party alone.

Friday night rolled around I and was so nervous that I couldn't figure out what to wear. I couldn't even remember the last time I went to a party that didn't involve my line of work. Finally, I decided on a short black dress with a low cut back held by spaghetti straps (a birthday present from Deedee). My hair was nicely put up with a few loose strands around my face and my black chocker around my neck finished off the look.

Anthony was at my door at 7:30 sharp. His eyes lit up and his slow easy smile was all over his face when he told me how great I looked. He raised my hand and turned me around for a complete view and the last angle of my turn landed me right into his arm where his lips were waiting for mine. The thought of bypassing the party crossed both of our mind but we couldn't do that to Stanley. We drove to the golf resort where the party was being held.

The room was filled with an older crowd and small group of young blood evenly spread out. I spotted Stanley facing the entrance talking to some of his associates in the far end of the room. I caught his attention and waved at him. He raised his glass toward us then went back to his conversation. Andrew was at the bar with three girls around him and as soon as he spotted me he rushed over with a hug and whispered 'perfect timing' in my ear. I looked over and watched the girls looking my way with jealous eyes. Andrew asked me to dance and told Anthony he needed to borrow me for a quick round. Before neither one of us could say yes he already had my hand and was leading me to the dance floor. As we danced, Andrew told me how he'd been trying to get away from those three girls for the past half hour. I teased him about his loyal groupies and he threatened not to compliment me on how nice I looked if I kept teasing him. As the music ended, I spotted Anthony with a brunette finishing their dance. I headed to the bar for a drink and before the bartender was back Anthony was right next to me. I grabbed my Absolute and cranberry and headed to the dance floor with Anthony. Later, I spotted Stanley who was busy making his rounds thanking everybody for coming. He finally came by for a quick hello and told me how nice it was of me to come and took me around introducing me to some of his friends and his brother who came in from England. We graced the dance floor with a short round then he went on hosting his party.

After a few trips to the bar I could feel a good buzz coming so I decided to work it off by spending the rest of the night dancing with the five most wanted bachelors in the room: Stanley, Andrew, Anthony, Jeremy and Donald.

Around midnight, Stanley got everyone's attention, thanked us one more time for the nice surprise and told us that his vampire days were over and that he was now "retiring to his pillow."

The party went on and before long most of the older guests were gone except for the few executive winos that were still left at the bar. My legs were killing me from standing and dancing in those new heels all night so I was grateful and ready when Anthony told me that we were leaving. I was looking forward to the drive home with Anthony but right before we got in his car, we spotted Andrew five cars down in the parking lot trying to get a wasted Donald and two giggly girls in his two seater Corvette; this was clearly an accident waiting to happen. Anthony walked over and after exchanging a few words came back to his car with Donald. Donald was one of those happy drunks, he kept trying to tell us jokes that really didn't make sense but the whole thing was so funny that you couldn't help but laugh. Anthony was telling him to keep his head out the window in case he had to throw up but Donald kept trying to convince us that he was okay. Although I didn't get the quiet and romantic time that I was hoping for I still had quite an entertaining ride home. It had been a fun but long night and a long hot shower with a good night sleep were my goals to complete the evening. Anthony walked me to my door and after a quick good night kiss, he had to rush back before Donald emptied his stomach in his Mercedes.

I was home for about half and hour and was just about to get in the shower when I heard someone at the door. I reached for my robe hoping that whoever it was would be gone by the time I reached the door. I looked through the pip hole and there stood Anthony. I quickly opened the door, hoping that nothing was wrong. Anthony stood there as if wondering whether to come in or not and all I could think of was how good he looked.

"Is everything okay?" I asked him. "Uh…there's something I've wanted to do for so long and…well…" I'm not sure what happen, but before he could finish his words our lips were pressed against each other's. He stopped and started to apologize but my lips didn't let him finish. My door was now closed with Anthony inside of my apartment, pressed against the entrance wall. I could feel his lips kissing my neck, my ears, and my chest. We slowly made it to the couch in the living room. I then realized that my robe, which before was covering my bare body, was somewhat open. I unwillingly stopped to fix my robe but his hands grabbed mine. He was now covering my body with kisses.

"Anthony," I said in between kisses, "I don't want things to change between us." "Why would they?" he asked. Just then I realized that my shower was still running. Forgetting his question, I headed toward the bathroom and said. "I was about to take a shower before you came by so—" "Would you mind if I joined you?" he asked before I could finish my sentence. I had forgotten what I was even talking about.

As hot as the water was, my nipples still managed to get hard from the excitement. His sign of arousal, which could be felt through his clothes earlier, was now visible to me. He washed me from head to toe before I returned the favor. The shower lasted longer than usual, but I enjoyed every second of it. As I finished rinsing off, he got out and dried off. When I was finished, he wrapped me up with a towel, carried me to the bedroom and placed me on my bed. He never bothered to dry me off, just re-wet me with his tongue. I was in some fantasy world when I felt him coming up towards my lips with his manhood in between my legs. "Anthony?" "What?" he whispered. "Is it gonna hurt?" I asked hesitantly. My question stopped him in the course of action as he sat back to look at me. I immediately regretted opening my mouth. "This is your first time?" he asked quietly. "Yes." I said. "I'm sorry if I should have said something sooner." He lay down next to me, both of us silent. "Are you sure you want to do this?" he asked. I laid thinking for what seemed an eternity. *Was I sure? I was about to lose my virginity to someone I truly adore and he's asking me if I 'm sure?* Without hesitation, I got on top of him, kissing every part of his beautiful body that my lips could find. As he understood my answer, he rolled me over his warm body lay on top of mine, his hands roaming continuously. The look in his eyes told me he needed this. Never having done this before, I was very nervous. I knew the basics, and some other things, but I lacked experience.

As the passions grew between us, I decided to use my knowledge to the fullest. As I moved down his body, his breathing became more rapid. I moved slowly kissing his steaming flesh, moving lower and lower until I reached his vulnerable point.

Almost oblivious to the moment, I took him into my mouth and did what I could. His hands ran through my hair, and over my neck. He began to breathe very loudly but suddenly pulled my head up to his and said, "Let's make love." He rolled me onto my back and mounted my shivering body. I just laid there, speechless, as he ran his hands over me. He began to move rhythmically, up and down. We were so close together. I could feel his heart beating. We moved in perfect rhythm now. I recall letting out a few yelps but the pain ripped through me for only a moment, then the pain was replaced with a pleasurable tingle.

His experience was very apparent. I certainly don't regret having him as my first. For what seemed like the sweetest eternity, he kissed my neck, my ears, and my face while moving up and down over and over with me.

I felt his thigh muscles tighten, as mine did too. He slowed as waves of pleasure rose throughout my limp body. He let out a long breath and lay his head upon my chest. Soundless, we laid there, kissing and holding each other. We whispered sweet nothings in each other's ears, and then we both fell asleep. We slept the whole night, close together. A long day ended in a good night's sleep.

CHAPTER 9

Danny's regular visit to the club, were turned into sessions of him trying to convince me to go out with him. Even with me telling him about my relationship with Anthony, he still persisted with these lame stories about how much he loved me and wanted to be with me. Deedee unfortunately was no help insisting that I give Danny a chance whether I loved Anthony or not. But how could I blame her; the word "monogamy" didn't exist in Deedee's vocabulary. Everyone knew that Danny didn't lack female companions. Perhaps he just got off on wanting what he couldn't have.

On a few occasions, Nick and Deedee would invite me to their football cookout or a day out on Nick's boat and strangely enough Danny would always find a way to be there. I knew that Deedee had something to do with it for she never failed to remind me of how much better off I'd be if I was Danny's girl. They've all tried to convince me how Danny would be willing to change if I was willing to give him a chance, but no matter how good he looks, Danny wasn't my type and I was very much in love with Anthony. Danny went through girls like underwear and I couldn't see him being in a monogamous or committed relationship no matter how much he claims to love me. I couldn't tell Nick who he could invite to his parties but I had no intention of letting him and Deedee mess what I had going on with Anthony. Danny was free to hold on to his ideas and dreams about us ending up together as long as he didn't try anything stupid or interfere with my relationship with Anthony in any kind of way. Danny would seize every chance he got to spoil me with presents and he would probably give me anything I asked for if I let him, in hope that I'd change my mind. The funny thing is that he really wasn't a bad guy. Apart from being involved in the wrong kind of business, a little short tempered at times and having no understanding of a committed relationship, he could be quite pleasant to hang with.

Anthony and I were in love. Our relationship was so close to perfection that it would scare me sometimes. Anthony was the kind of man that made you dream of being a better person. Sometimes I'd feel guilty for not telling him about my job, especially when I had to make up excuses on why sometimes I couldn't see him or go out with him, but I kept telling myself that I'd find a normal job before he could find out. The problem was that between school, my two jobs, and my lack of dedication, finding that other job didn't seem like it was gonna happen anytime soon.

With school starting, my load was getting a lot heavier than I bargained for. Right before Stanley went back to England, I talked him into letting me work on the same days that I worked at the club since I was usually done at the office by 3:30 and didn't have to be at the club until 8:00 P.M., this way I wouldn't have to keep going to the office with a headache from my hangovers and would free up some time for me and Anthony, at least until I could figure something out. Anthony would sometimes come over to help me with my homework but we would spend most of the time in each other's arm or under the covers studying everything but law. Finally we agreed on me studying by myself and if I really needed help, to meet at the library but even there we'd find ourselves in the deep corners of the library behind the oversized shelves exploring things that were meant to be studied and explored in a human anatomy or sex ed class.

Sometime around the end of April, Deedee got her green card. After eight years of not seeing her family, she decided to fly back home to Argentina. The Friday night before she left, business was really slow at the club. I'd never made less than $200.00 on a Friday but that night I barely had $80.00 and only one hour to go. I was in the dressing room freshening up my make-up when Deedee came in and asked me to work a private party with her after work.

These private parties were the hidden skeletons of the club. Most of the girls didn't even know about them, some had ideas and the ones that did know could not and would not talk about it because they were part of it. This last group, known as the house girls, were carefully chosen by the manager because they had to be trusted. I never got to participate in those private parties but through Deedee I more or less knew or thought I knew what went on.

"You're sure you want me to work the party?" I asked her. "Yes, we're short a girl and Larry wanted me to ask you so you could work in my spot since I'm gonna be gone for a while," she replied. "I'm sorry Deedee but I don't think I wanna get involve in…" Before I could finish Deedee cut in with an "I-don't-have-time-for-this-crap" attitude. "Look Angel, you really don't have a choice. Some girls have to beg Larry to work these parties so trust me he's just being nice asking you. If you want to say no you better go do it yourself and make sure you have a damn good reason why, otherwise start looking for another club to work because things might stop being as smooth as they've been."

I looked at Deedee and realized that she had a good buzz going on but for some reason I don't think her warnings were from the alcohol. I was already having a bad night and I was in no mood to deal with any shit. I'd been here for almost three years so if Larry wanted to give me crap for not wanting to work some party he could kiss my ass." As I turned to walk out of the room and go talk to Larry, I caught my reflection in the walled mirror and thought, "who was I fooling, getting all offended because Larry told me to work a private drug party, and where do I get the audacity thinking I was better than the girls that did. As my father used to say, "You hang around dogs long enough you bound to get fleas." Somewhere along the road I became someone other than the small town girl on the way to becoming a lawyer. After three years of dancing, drinking, partying with these people, how could I expect them to see me in any other way other than being one of them.

I stood there for a moment and then with defeat in my voice I turned to Deedee and said "Whatever, I could use the cash." "It's not that bad," Deedee said as she pulled her cigarette out of her boots. Feeling some of my desperation she grabbed my hand, dragged me out the dressing room as she yelled "We're gonna get fucked up tonight!! Yeah!"

Deedee was definitely crazy. Once again that night I decided I was gonna do whatever it takes to get the hell out of this business.

It was 3:00 A.M. when the party crew started coming. From the look of them one would assumed they were regular customers. They came one by one and slowly made their way to the Champagne Room, which on those days, was closed to the regular customers after 2:00 A.M. Normally, the club would shut down exactly at 3:00 A.M. All the girls except for those working the party had to be gone and if questions were asked the answer was always "a private bachelor party."

That night, once the doors were closed at 3:00 A.M., the music was put back on, the bar reopened and in the Champagne Room were some of the most powerful drug dealers partying with their friends or cutting deals with their associates. Eight girls usually worked the party, and by the time Deedee and I joined them, joints, lines of cocaine and glasses of whiskey were all over the room. As the manager introduced me as the new house girl, Deedee tactfully whispered in my ear "See no evil, hear no evil."

The girls seemed to know the routine; they were already attending to the needs of the guys. An older man was sitting in the corner table in deep conversation with a younger bald headed guy. Two were sipping on Budweiser and by their looks they were obviously the bodyguards. The other five men were busy on one of the couches with their lines, their joints and whatever girl was with them. Deedee told me there were ten of them so obviously one was missing. I looked toward the end of the room and on the other couch behind the two girls dancing were one set of white heels and two sets of men's feet. As the girls bent over to give a closer view of her anatomy I matched the three sets of feet to Larry, Danny and one of the girl's sitting on Danny's lap. For some reason my heart tighten, I know Danny could be anybody's customer if he wanted to, but the sight of a girl kissing all over him just rubbed me the wrong way. Deedee as drunk as she was read my mind, she walked passed me and whispered "jealous?" I was gonna turn to give her an answer but then Larry called me over and made room for me on the crowded couch next to Danny as he loudly introduced me as "their new Angel." The guys looked over to where we were and whistled.

With everything going on, I was feeling very uncomfortable. Some of the girls were taking turns doing lines and giving blowjobs. Deedee was in the corner with a joint with one of the guys feeling on her breast and I was hearing things, which I'm sure I shouldn't be hearing. This was way over my head.

I got two glasses of champagne down as fast as I could, held a third in my hand and ordered a double shot of cognac. I had to be wasted for this shit. Danny was getting wasted with me sitting on one side and Montana, the girl from before who was kissing all over him on the other side of him. Just then Rolly, the big boss, proposed a toast to the crew with samples from his new shipment of marijuana. Randy the DJ and Karen the bartender were turning brown from kissing so much of Rolly's fat ass. They took the samples to pass them out and Rolly grabbed three and brought them to our couch. Montana and Danny took theirs and I without thinking said "no thanks" as I lifted my glass of Champagne to indicate that I was fine. The room somehow got all quiet and Rolly gave me this questioning look that made me realize that I might have made a mistake and felt obligated to justify my answer. "Hey," I said trying to sound in control "let me get this glass down then I'll take you up on the offer." Danny, feeling the tension and stares, tilted toward my face and caught me with my mouth open as he went in for a kiss, stopped, grabbed the joint from Rolly then said "that's my homegirl, we normally share" then brought me to his lips for a much longer kiss. When he finally let me pull away from him Rolly was back at his table talking to some of the other guys but still somewhat looking toward us, his gaze met ours, and he gave us a wink and took a long hit from his sample. Everything happened so fast that I didn't know whether to smack Danny for kissing me or thank him for saving my butt.

Before I could come back to the moment and figure out what just happened or even finish my glass, Deedee called me over to dance with her for the guy she'd been sitting with. She was so wasted I couldn't believe she was still functioning. As we danced she started touching me, and kissing on my neck, my breast, my stomach for some strange reason it didn't seem like a performance and definitely did not feel like one to me. I didn't even know how to react. As the song ended the applause from behind us made me realize that we had an audience. It was the weirdest feeling; it's as if I was outside of my body yet watching myself in this mess. The part of me watching was angry with Danny for kissing me, Deedee for her so-called "performance" and especially at myself for getting into this. I got off the table and asked the bartender for a couple of shots of Tequila I really wanted to get drunk and for some reason I just couldn't. It's as if part of me wanted to register what was going on to the fullest. Finally the night was over. Between tips, commissions and what we got paid for the party, Deedee made close to $2,000.00 and I about $1,200.00. On our way home, I felt compelled to talk to Deedee about her so-called performance but there was so much more I wanted to know about this party business. Part of me was still mad at what happened that night but the new me, which lately I'd been trying to understand, was thinking how great it was to have a thousand plus dollars sitting in my pocket so since it was our last night working together for a while I decided to just let it go.

"You know you'll have to work all the other parties?" said Deedee breaking the silence of the early morning ride. "The hell I do," I said glancing over at her. "You can't start and decide that you don't want to do it anymore, that's why only certain girls get to work those parties." "Who are these guys anyway?"

By the time Deedee was done telling the story behind the men from the party I was wishing I didn't ask. These men were mostly drug dealers as suspected and the side group such as Tim was a police officer, K-9 to be exact. Thomas, the guy that was sitting with Deedee was a lawyer and the two bodyguards were ex-convicts. Rolando (Rolly) was the big boss that everything had to go through. He was one of the biggest kingpins around and the other guys were his associates. These parties were usually arranged at the club every other

month. Once in a while, they would take place in hotel suites or some well furnished empty house. As Deedee went on talking I sank deep into the passenger
seat wondering what I'd gotten myself into.

The week after Deedee left, my life started to crumble. Anthony and I were
shopping at Bloomingdales and thankfully Anthony was to the side looking
through some shirts, when Marco one of my customers approached me. "Hey
Angel," he shouted in his loud Cuban voice. "Hey, Marco," "How's work?" he
asked. I was hoping he'd say hi and leave but he started asking me about the
other girls. As Anthony headed toward me, my heart started pounding but
Marco finally decided to say goodbye. "What was that all about?" asked
Anthony. "Old acquaintance," I said, hoping that he couldn't hear the tension
in my voice. As we finished our shopping my mind was running around wondering if Anthony was gonna ask any more questions, and what I would say. It
wasn't until we were driving home that he asked me about Marco. "Why did
that guy call you Angel?" The question caught me off guard since I didn't'
think or was hoping that he'd missed the conversation with Marco. Trying to
remain calm I quickly lied, "Oh, he probably mixed up my name with someone else's." Anthony dropped me off, with no further questions. That night I
decided I was gonna tell him about my job next time we were together.

A couple of days later, Anthony got a call from his father requesting his
assistance in this high profile case that was going on in England. The day
before he left we were so busy making love and complaining how much we
were going to miss each other that I decided to wait until he was back from his
trip to tell him about my job. Who knows, maybe by then I'd find another job.
He spent the night at my place and early the next morning, I drove him to the
airport. It was so hard to think that I wouldn't see him for at least two weeks;
it's as if he was going away for good. We were standing at the gate waiting in
line for him to board when I spotted Nick and Danny walking towards us in a
hurry. I tried to look away hoping that the three people ahead would hurry up
so Anthony could go in before they could reach us or maybe they'd be in too
much of a hurry to spot me. But, fat chance. "Hey mama, what you doing
here?" asked Nick as he placed a kiss on either side of my face. Danny and I had
not talked since that kissing incident so I was hoping he'd just stand there as if
I didn't know him but he followed Nick with the kiss on both checks with an
awkward air between us.

I told them that I was dropping my boyfriend off as I reached for Anthony's
hand. Nick extended his hand and said, "You must be the Anthony I've heard
so much about you." Anthony shook his hand with a smile that only I could

tell was forced for the occasion and replied, as he looked at me "all good things I hope." Feeling trapped with the situation I went ahead with the introduction. "Oh, I'm sorry guys where are my manners, Anthony, this is Nick, Deedee's boyfriend and that's his friend Danny," the whole time avoiding Danny's look. They shook hands and before anything could be said, Anthony said he had to board the plane. We kissed goodbye and he told me he'd call me that night. As much as I wanted him to call suddenly I knew he was gonna ask questions about Nick and Danny.

That night I went to work, forgot my cell phone at home, and ended up missing Anthony's call.

CHAPTER 10

It was 8:00 A.M. my time the next morning when my phone rang. My head was still pounding from my excess drinking at work the night before and the sun shinning through my windows was not helping. When I managed to say hello I realized it was Anthony on the other end.

The pounding in my head was louder than my voice and as much as I missed him and wanted to talk to him the bad reception of our phones was making my head hurt even more. I apologized for missing his call and told him some lie about going on campus to a study group for an upcoming test and forgetting my cell phone at home. I'm not sure if he believed me but he didn't say anything for a moment then out of the blue he said, "you know your friends that we ran into at the airport?" Right away my heart started galloping keeping up with the rhythm of the pounding headache. "What about them?" I asked. "I'm not sure why," he continued "but one of them looked familiar, not like I know him or anything but like I've seen him somewhere…" "I don't know what to tell you honey," I said, hoping he'd drop the subject but he didn't. "How do you know them?" he asked.

"I met them through Deedee but I really don't know much about them" I said quickly. "Well, he continued, I'm sure it'll come to me."

Hoping to change the subject I asked how Stanley was doing, the time frame of the case they were working on, and then I told him about all the homework I had to work on. After expressing how much we were missing each other, we said our goodbyes.

My mind and body were finally getting the hang of working at two different place, and with Anthony and Deedee being away my social life was now nonexistent, so my plan was to work as much as possible for the two weeks that

Anthony was gonna be gone and quit right before he gets back but of-course things didn't work out that way.

A few days after Anthony left, Danny came to the club. I was doing a table dance for a customer but the minute I spotted him I'd decided that I didn't want to deal with him, I just didn't have the energy. It didn't take long before the bartender came by and told me that Danny was in the Champagne Room waiting for me; but after the private dance the customer asked me if I wanted something to drink to which I gratefully accepted hoping to buy time before going to tell Danny that I couldn't sit with him tonight. I was soon called to go on stage and as I finished my performance, I watched the customer that I was sitting with wave goodbye pointing to his watch indicating that he had to go. Danny was standing at the entrance of the Champagne Room looking at me with Larry standing next to him. "Fuck" I thought "now I had to find a good excuse to stay away from Danny or Larry was gonna be mad at me for neglecting one of his top customers." I got off the stage and made my rounds and decided to just go and sit with him for a while or at least until Larry leaves for the night which should be soon since the night manager was already here and no private parties were scheduled. Larry excused himself to go to the office as soon as I came in and here I was, left by myself with Danny. A bottle of Champagne was being chilled on the table with two empty glasses. I sat on the couch thinking I've been in this business long enough that I could bullshit if I have to so since I'm here I might as well make the money and get it over with.

I was going along, making conversation when he placed his beer down and as if in disbelief he asked if I was mad at him for something. "I don't know Danny, should I be mad at you for something?" I asked sarcastically. "Angel," he said looking at me like he was starting to get mad, "I don't have time for the bullshit just tell me what's up." "Bullshit?" I replied trying to keep my cool "you kissed me and never even apologized and you don't think I should be upset." "Apologize for what? For saving your ass? You should be thanking me, if anything." "You know what Danny, fuck you," I said as I got off the couch. "I'd love to baby but it seems like Anthony's got that job," he responded in mockery. I stopped dead in my tracks when I heard Anthony's name. I turned around ready to explode and found Danny inches behind me, so close that I could feel his breath. "Leave Anthony out of this," I said looking at him dead in the eye.

I left the Champagne Room, walked right into Larry's office and told him that I had to go home. He just asked me if I was working tomorrow and thankfully didn't ask me why I wanted to leave. I got home on pilot mode in less than half an hour. My stomach was telling me I should eat but I just didn't have the appetite or the will. I looked in the refrigerator, grabbed the box of Frosted Flakes, and filled a bowl with milk and cereal as I filled up my tub with hot water. That night I sat in the living room watching the Three Stooges, thinking of the night Anthony and I watched those same videos, wishing that my life was different. I was feeling so alone when the phone rang; nobody except for Larry knew I was home so, I thought I'd let the answering machine pick it up. Then I heard Anthony's voice telling me how much he was missing me. I grabbed the receiver just in time and although he had intended to leave a message he ended up talking for hours and as we talked and laughed in between scenes of The Three Stooges my loneliness made its way in the back of my mind.

CHAPTER 11

It's been almost two weeks since Deedee and Anthony left, Spring term was over for school and I was working all day and most of the night. Sometimes if Anthony wasn't going to call or had called early enough I'd work a double shift. Whether I wanted to admit it or not, my work/drinking/eating habits were clearly taking a toll on me. My health was deteriorating, my schoolwork was suffering and my state of loneliness was becoming a norm.

That Friday of the second week I made it to the office and barely made it to my afternoon summer class. By the time I made it home, I was covered with sweat from the chills that had been hurting me all day. I got in bed thinking I'd rest for an hour before heading to work at the Unicorn but my alarm never went off. When I got up to use the bathroom it was 3:30 A.M. and I was still in my clothes. I knew Larry was gonna be mad for missing work on a Friday night but at this point there was nothing I could do. I picked up the phone, called the "Unicorn" and told the night shift manager that I'd be at work tomorrow and would work a double to make up for tonight.

Anthony's trip was prolonged for a few more days and Deedee was due that Sunday so with nothing better to do on a beautiful Saturday, I headed for work. I brought a sandwich just to make sure I'd have something to eat and as promised worked a double shift. About 2:30 A.M. when the DJ announced that the club would be closing in half an hour I was so drunk and tired that I just assumed it was the regular 4:30 A.M. closing time. After the announcement, Larry came by and told me that he needed to see me in the office. The sight of Larry being here at this time of night usually indicated that a private party was on the way. I knew what he was gonna ask me but my body was telling me it had enough. As much as I pleaded with Larry, he wouldn't let me go home and since most of the girls were already gone he just told me that I didn't have a choice. I made my way to the dressing room, with every inch of my body aching. I opened the small refrigerator that was recently added in the dressing room for the girls and grabbed the sandwich that I brought from home hoping that I'd feel better once I had something in my stomach. This party was slightly different from the previous one I did; only four girls including myself were working filling the spot as waitress, dancer, and as usual whatever else was needed for the night. It was obvious that a deal was going through because once the men (Rolly, Nick, Danny, Jerry, Tim and two unknown guys) were served their drinks, they remained in the Champagne Room talking while we sat at the main bar drinking and entertaining a couple of Rolly's associates who for whatever reasons were not involved in the discussion. After about an hour, we were called in for table dances and body shots. The two unknown guys dressed in black leather jackets left right after our first table dance carrying two black briefcases in each hand. The party had now officially started. The tables were instantly filled with lines of cocaine, the room filled up with smoke from the joints and Rolly's table was packed with sample bags of all kinds of colorful pills. From the joyful moods and expression from the guys, especially Rolly, it was obvious that the deal must have went well. I was still mad at Danny so I was trying to stay clear of him. The guys started mixing different kinds of pills in the different glasses and passing them around. The four of us girls were standing on two stools dancing when we got ours, we each carefully held our glass waiting for Rolly's toast the whole time my head is screaming "you don't wanna do this" but I did, I watched myself gulped the mixes and cheered with the other three girls hoping to not stand out.

I was so fucked up that I'm not sure what happened after that. I remember walking to my car and Danny trying to grab my keys from me and from there I must have blacked out. I woke up in an unknown place in this huge heated waterbed. My head was pounding and my heart was beating too fast and too loud. I managed to open my eyes and spotted three pictures on a dresser across from the bed. Danny with his Mom, Danny with a little boy and the same little boy in a cowboy Halloween costume. "This must be Danny's place" I thought, I wanted to get up but the motion of the bed was making me sick so I decided to stay still. I looked down and felt a hint of relief at the sight of my clothes on my body. "Hopefully he didn't try anything," I thought. Feeling a little bit cold, I tried to reach the cover that lay slightly out of reach when Danny walked in with a cup of coffee in hand. "Are you up?" he asked. "I think so," I answered holding on to my head. "What happened," I asked him as he placed the coffee cup on the dresser. "You had a bad mix," he said looking down at me. I wanted to sit up and find out what happened but remembering I was mad at him I didn't wanna ask him for help. He must have read my mind. That cocky smile of his filled his face as he extended his hand and said, "How's your head?" I reluctantly grabbed his hand and said, "It's been better."

I sat on the edge of his bed and asked him to tell me how I ended up at his place. Apparently, I had more than one type of mix with those pills and with minimal amount of food, my body couldn't handle it so I blacked out right before I got in my car. When I asked him for the time, it was 5:15 P.M. "Shit, I was supposed to go to the office this morning and go to school for a group presentation" "Angel," he said with a perplexed smile on his face "it's Sunday, how can you have school?" "It's Sunday? I repeated, "Oh my goodness I'm losing it." I tried to get up but the fast movement made the room spin and my legs almost gave out on me. Danny caught me and sat me on the side of the bed. "I have to get home," I told him but he insisted on my eating something before I leave. He walked me to his kitchen, sat me in one of the kitchen chairs and started to make an omelet. I didn't think anything happened between us but I wanted to make sure. We were both quiet for a while then as he placed the omelets on the table for us to eat I decided to ask him. He took one look at me and I knew he was pissed. "I stopped you from driving off and killing yourself and that's the fucking thanks I get…you actually think I'd do some shit like that? What kind of a man do you take me for?" "Danny…I'm sorry." "Whatever," he said in a more calmed voice as he shook his head, "you can tell Anthony or whatever the fuck his name is that nothing happened." He took his plate to the living room turned on the TV leaving me at the kitchen table. I pushed my chair back thinking I'd go and talk to him but his voice came in louder than he realized telling me that his shower was next to his bedroom. I really wanted to get home before Anthony called me but I suddenly realized how bad I smelled with the funk of cigarettes, sweat and alcohol. While in the shower I started feeling bad for giving Danny such a hard time. It was clear that I hurt his feelings and as the pounding of my head reminded me of my condition, I thought of where I could have been if Danny didn't stop me from driving last night. I changed into one of Danny's oversized sweats, which he had on top of the towels for me and went back to his living room. He was still sitting on his couch staring at the TV. "Danny?" He looked up from the screen and I simply said "Thank you, and I'm really sorry for…"

He didn't let me finish, he just said, "you're lucky I like you, otherwise your ass would be walking to the Unicorn to get your car." The tone of his voice seemed less tense than before and I took that as his way of accepting my apology.

Danny drove me back to my car, which was parked, at the club. The moment we got on the road I fell asleep and did not wake up until his sudden stop in the Unicor's parking lot. By the time I got home that early evening I had the chills, a nasty cough, and a fever. Deedee called to tell me about her trip but my mind couldn't stay focused for more than 10 minutes. She was so broke from her trip that she was planning on working every night to make up for the cost of the trip. The few days that followed I couldn't find the energy or the appetite to eat anything. Deedee came by a few times but she was so tired from the long working hours that she was always in a hurry to either go to sleep or go see Nick. I'd lie in bed hoping I'd fall asleep except my coughing kept waking me up. Every time Anthony would call I'd try to cheer up and tell him that I just had a cold so he wouldn't worry. With me not getting better Deedee decided to play doctor, she came by with all kind of flu and cold medicine and stayed with me for a couple of days, forcing me to have her chicken soup which she swore was the answer to any disease.

The next time I spoke to Anthony, I found out that their case was gonna be longer than expected so, for the time being, Anthony promised to commute back and forth between London and Miami so we could have the weekend together. A few days elapsed and by the time Anthony was due back, I was up and running.

Friday night I watched him come into the building and before he could even knock, I opened the door running into his arms. I'd never missed him so much and apparently he'd missed me too. We wanted to be alone and catch up on the past two and a half weeks so we drove to The Eden Rock Hotel and spent the weekend making love and ordering room service. Monday morning was bittersweet when Anthony had to pack and head back to England, but at least I knew he was gonna be back the following Friday night.

I was on cloud nine when I got home Monday morning. My mind was still thinking about my weekend with Anthony when I spotted the blinking light of the answering machine. The first message was Deedee telling me to call her, the second was Danny checking if I was okay, the third and forth was Deedee sounding either way over the heel excited or freaking out about something which apparently she couldn't say over the phone. I had to get to the office so I quickly changed and figured I'd call her while driving. I was just about to walk out the door when the phone rang. I picked up the phone and sure enough it was Deedee on the other end. "Hey," I said before she could say anything "I'm just walking out the door so call me on my cell." "Bitch" she said jokingly "I just need a minute," before I could say anything she blurted "I got engaged." "What? Deedee, when did this happen?" "Saturday night...ooh I'm so excited I'll have to tell you the details tonight, are you working?" I wasn't sure what I was doing tonight I hadn't worked for almost a week and being sober kind of felt good although I had to admit I missed the money. "I don't know Deedee, I'll call you before I go to class."

My day at the office was so hectic that I didn't even get a chance to go on my break. Two of the secretaries were out for the day and Stanley's old secretary, who had just returned from her vacation, was backed up with work from the two weeks that she was out. By the time I left for my afternoon classes, I was running late and starving which left me no time to call Deedee. As I drove home early that evening, I tried to call her hoping we could have dinner because I was dying to hear about her engagement but she didn't answer. After trying a couple of times both at her house and her cell phone, I left her a message and decided to go home and call it a day.

Tuesday morning I was awakened by Anthony's call, phoning to let me know that he made it okay and how much he was missing us being together. Later that day I was working on my homework when I realized that Deedee hadn't called me back. "I hoped she didn't run off and get married without me," I thought. I dialed her cell phone, which rang and rang for a while before it finally transferred to her voice mail. I hung up and called her house, which also rang for a while before a sleepy Deedee answered on the other end.

"Where the hell have you been?" I asked her, relieved that she answered. "I'm sorry" she barely managed to say "I was gonna call you but I didn't get home till 6:00 A.M. and I'm just about dead." "Six?" I repeated in disbelief "did you fly to Las Vegas to get married last night?" I said somewhat jokingly. "No" she answered "Nick needed an extra hand last night so I had to fill in."

We were both silent for a split moment, Deedee and I have known each other long enough to know and understand when further questions could not be asked and the mentioning of Nick's name could only mean one thing, "a drug deal" which would classify this conversation in the "no more questions" category. "Are you working today?" I asked her. "Yeah," she answered as she yawned "let me get a couple of hours of shut eye then I'll come by, we can chill for a bit before we go to work."

Late that afternoon when Deedee walked though my door all excited I couldn't wait to hear about her engagement. My first reaction was excitement then once we stopped the screaming, jumping and hugging the thought of

Louis came to mind. "Deedee, what are you gonna do about Louis?" "The only thing I can do," she said with determination in her voice "make that fucker sign the divorce papers because (extending her hand with the engagement ring towards me) I'm getting ma-a-a-rried!"

With Deedee around it didn't take me long to get back in my party mode. We went to this local Mexican restaurant for lunch and loaded up on the margaritas then drove to work with a full stomach and a nice buzz in celebration of Deedee's engagement. The celebration continued throughout the night as Deedee's customers kept the drinks and the shots coming for the occasion. For a Tuesday night the bar was pretty packed and with hardly any girls on the floor, it was an easy moneymaking night.

At 4:30 A.M., Deedee and I both drunk as skunks were on our way home in her BMW. Deedee, after smoking her last joint for the night, was snoozing on the passenger side, leaving me as the driver. The streets were more or less empty and some of them still dark from the absence of the power lines. I was feeling a little drowsy so I woke Deedee up to keep me company. She sat up and started telling me a joke, the kind that required a good high or buzz for it to be funny. I was listening as I tried to focus on the road ahead since my vision was somewhat blurry from my drinking and Deedee was just about to get to the punch line when the flashing lights appeared in the rearview mirror. I knew I had to stop but for some strange reason I just couldn't. Fuck! I shouted. I wanted to cry but strangely enough I started laughing uncontrollably, "You have to stop! Samantha! Stop" cried Deedee. But I couldn't, my mind could not register the concept of having to brake. Deedee jerked the steering wheel from me and swerved and after a double spin crashed right into the side railing of the road.

"Oh shit Deedee your car!" I exclaimed as the air bags halfway deployed into our faces. "Fuck the car," said Deedee, "your ass is drunk." "Shit, shit, shit" she cried. "I'm better at this shit, quick, let's switch places." We were half way through the switch when we realized that it was too late, the officer was already near the back bumper. By then my laughing stage was over, I was now crying. Deedee was pinching me on the side signaling me to stop but I couldn't. "Are we okay in there?" he asked. Deedee quickly answered, "Yes sir we're okay."

Ignoring Deedee's response he pointed his flashlight toward me and said "Ma'am, did you realize you were swerving all over the road?" "I'm sorry officer, we saw something crossing and we were trying to miss it," Deedee explained as I continued to sob somewhat quietly. The officer didn't seem to be interested in what Deedee had to say, he bent over closer to me and said, "Can

I see your driver's license and the registration for the car?" Deedee handed me my wallet from her glove compartment along with the registration, which I handed over. The officer went back to his car.

"Stop crying, you're only gonna make things worse," Deedee said in a low but stern voice. "For goodness sake you've never been pulled over before?"

I don't think she wanted an answer to her question but I heard myself answering her. "No." "Damn girl, what are you, mother fucking Theresa?..." The officer was back in sight coming towards the car and another police car with two officers was pulling behind the first one. "Just shut up," Deedee said under her breath "I'll do the talking." The officer flashed his bright lights in my face again and told me to step out the car, which I barely managed to do. The just arrived officer approached me and mentioned something about a substance test. By now both of them were standing with a pad and pen watching me waddling and making a fool of myself. I did the Breathalyzer test and was about to do some stupid line test when I heard a car door slam behind me. I turned around and the quick movement landed me right on my butt on the pavement. From the floor, I spotted Deedee heading towards us with her blouse open more than it was before, showing more cleavage than she needed to. "Get back in the car," shouted one of the officers, but Deedee kept coming as if she didn't hear him.

"Ma'am we need you to get back in your vehicle, Ma'am, Ma'am you need to get back" too late, Deedee was already next to me. "Has your friend been partying?" asked one of the other officers. "Not exactly." answered Deedee. "She just had a glass of wine and I guess since it was her first time it kind of went to her head. I'm really sorry officer. It's my car and I should have been driving."

Deedee was telling the officer some story about her being responsible for letting me drive but I was so freaked out with this whole thing that I couldn't register what she was saying. Before I knew it she was arguing with the officer about her taking the Breathalyzer test. I was now handcuffed and placed in the back seat of one the officer's cars, and then they followed Deedee to the BMW for her ID. I waited and sweated like a pig for what seemed like an eternity. Finally two officers came back and told me that they were gonna take me in. They rolled up slowly next to the BMW where Deedee was leaning against the damaged car talking to the other officer. When she saw me, she came to my window and said, "It'll be okay mama."

I wanted to ask her what was going on but just like the idea of me going to jail couldn't sink in, the words couldn't come out. They drove me away as I looked out the window with tears running down my face.

I was placed in a cold room filled with women from all walks of life. As we stood waiting to be booked, others lined the three benches contouring the room. It's funny how quick going to jail can sober up a person; I was wide-awake trying to absorb everything. Some of the women in the room were talking, some were snoozing and I was in a corner dreading the thoughts of the stories that I'd often heard about prison life. The booking process started, people were being called one at a time. We were each allowed one-phone call but with only two phones at our disposal, it seemed like it was taking forever. As I waited, it suddenly dawned on me that I didn't know whom to call. Deedee was the only person I could think of but I didn't even know where she was, for all I knew she was probably in jail too. I wanted to cry but was too scared to. My mind started to wonder and analyze things; I couldn't believe that the same girl that came here from Georgia to become a lawyer was now in jail with a bunch of prostitutes, drunks and God knows what, if dad could see me now…I'd been standing for so long that my legs were now going numb; my anger and shame were raising my heart rate. I slowly sank to the floor, rested my head on my knees and decided to just let it be. The sound of my name startled me, I answered and headed toward the officer standing in the doorway. "Follow me please," she said with indifference in her voice. I followed her to a room and found Danny talking to an officer over the counter. As I continued to walk toward the counter Danny came toward me and said "Everything's taking care of, you're going home."

I couldn't believe what I was hearing. We walked to his car and as soon as we got on the road my composure was gone and I just broke down and started crying. Danny kept rubbing my shoulder and telling me it was okay but I wouldn't stop crying. He pulled me over to his side and held me in his arms. "How did you know I was here?" I asked him when I was finally able to talk. "Deedee called and told me what happened." "Where is she? Is she okay?" I asked. "Yes" he said "She's fine, she's with Nick."

With Deedee on probation and the way she was running her mouth I wondered how she escaped going to jail but with so many other things to worry about I was just happy that we were both okay. We got to the apartment and unfortunately Deedee was with Nick and my stuff was with her so I couldn't get in. Danny tried calling Nick but no answer so finally we decided to go his place. "Can I get you anything?" he asked as he headed straight for the kitchen.

I sank myself on his couch and asked him for some coffee. As the coffee brewed he turned on the TV and came and sat next to me. "Danny, would it be possible for me to use your shower?"

I stood under the water as I scrubbed and cried about my helpless, out of control life. I knew I needed help but for some reason I felt trapped and way over my head in this new life that I'd created for myself. I'm not sure how long I was in there but when Danny knocked on the door I looked up and realized how foggy the room had gotten from the steam of the water. I grabbed a towel, wrapped it around me and told him to come in. He peeped his head inside and just asked if I was okay. I asked him if I could borrow something clean to put on and he teased and said as long as I promised to return it. He was referring to the fact that I still hadn't returned his sweats from the last time.

We sat on his couch drinking coffee, beeping Deedee and waiting for her to call back. It was now 2:00 P.M. and I hadn't slept all day. With everything going on I forgot to call the office and tell them I wasn't coming in. It was obvious that I wasn't gonna make it to school and my body was ready to collapse. Danny was mostly on the phone and in between we'd talk about the incident or why Deedee or Nick wasn't calling back. I must have fallen asleep, because I was awakened by the strong smell of marijuana with a cover over me. Danny and Deedee, the source of the smell were sitting across from me talking to Nick who was finishing a line of coke. Deedee came next to me, gave me a hug and asked me if I was okay. "I think so," I answered.

"We ordered some Chinese food, it should be here in a minute," she said. The thought of Chinese food made me realize how hungry I was. "What happened to you?" I asked her. Deedee explained that during the incident they found out that there was a warrant for her arrest so she had to go to court today to clear it up. I thought normally they'd take you in if you have a warrant for your arrest but this was South Florida and the law sometimes seems to work differently depending on whom you know. I asked her if she brought my bag with her and she told me it was in the car along with my cell phone, which has been ringing off the hook. "Do you know who was calling?" I asked hoping that it wasn't Anthony but Deedee told me that she didn't look and that she got tired of the phone ringing and finally turned it off.

By the time I got home it was nearly 7:00 P.M.; my home answering machine along with my cell phone was loaded with messages from the office, Stanley and Anthony making sure I was okay. I'm not sure why but for some reason I decided to call Stanley first, two rings later the phone was picked up by Anthony who was at his dad's at the time. Caught off guard I was somewhat speechless. The conversation that followed wasn't the sweet late night talk that we usually had. Of course, he wanted to know what happened, my mind was racing debating how much of what happened could be told without blowing up my cover.

"I'm sorry for worrying you guys so much, Deedee and Nick got engaged and we had a girl's night out to celebrate. Unfortunately I forgot my phone at home and had a little too much to drink so I had to spend the night at her place." By the time I got around to asking to talk to Stanley, Anthony had gone from being worried and relieved to being upset and paternal, telling me how I should be more responsible and should look into getting help for my drinking. I know he'd call a few times where I was too wasted or hung over to have a coherent conversation and my drinking problem was no news to me but after spending a night in jail, how irresponsible I was, was the last thing I wanted to hear. Stanley apparently wasn't home so with all the tension in the air I decided to bring our conversation to an end then poured myself a strong one and sank in bed feeling sorry for myself.

Thursday morning I woke up feeling under the weather with every inch of my body aching. I had my final assignment along with a few late assignments that needed to be completed and I was wondering how I was gonna get them done. I packed a bag to go to the library hoping that a change in my surrounding would help my motivation. On my way out the door, I grabbed the stack of mail that had been sitting on my counter thinking I'd go through them at the library. As I drove around the library parking lot looking for a shaded spot, some of the mail slipped off the passenger's seat and landed on the floor. The envelope with the orange and green emblem caught my attention; it was a letter from school. I couldn't think of any upcoming school event that would generate courtesy mail. Forgetting about the shade, I pulled in the nearest parking spot and reluctantly opened the envelope. Something in my gut told me that it was bad news and this time I was right. The letter informed me that I was placed on academic probation due to my grade point average which was under observation from the previous semester, since my current GPA wasn't much of an improvement, not to mention my excessive absence from school, I was being told to set an appointment to see an academic advisor before I could register for the Fall semester. I guess there was no point in going to the library to do anything anymore. I balled up the letter and threw it at the windshield and started pounding on my steering wheel as tears flowed down my face. I wanted to scream at somebody but I had no one to blame but myself. Without even thinking I drove to Deedee's. My body was acting all weird; I was freezing and sweating at the same time. As I pulled in her parking lot, the sight of the dent in her car reinforced how much of a failure I was. I checked my face in the mirror making sure there was no sign that I'd been crying before leaving my car.

Deedee was back to her happy self, which was nice to see. She took one look at me and knew that something was bothering me. As usual she wanted to know what was going on but it was so nice to see her happy again that I didn't want to cloud her day with my problems. She'd just finished her laundry so I joined in folding and putting away her clothes. "You just missed Larry's call," she said as we stopped for a cold one. "Did you tell him about what happened?" I asked. "Nah...he just wanted to make sure that we were gonna be at work tomorrow night," which meant we had a party to work.

"Deedee," I said with a heavy tone as I stared at the half full beer bottle "I can't...I really don't want to. "I, I don't think I can do this anymore." "What the fuck is this?" Deedee asked with worries in her voice "Your goodbye speech?" "Deedee come on, even if I wanted to I couldn't anyway, tomorrow is Friday and Anthony is coming back, I can't just disappear for the night." Deedee's eyes rested on me as she took a long sip then said, "All right girl, I'll cover for you but you gotta tell me what's going on." "I've just got a lot on my mind" I told her. "Whatever it is it's wearing you down, because you look like shit." "Did you find out how much it'd cost for the damage on your car?" I asked her trying to change the subject.

"This shop down the street said about $7,600 but I think I can find some place cheaper," Deedee said. Then without a pause she asked, "Now what's going on?" I started telling her about my feeling under the weather, my situation with school, my court situation for my DUI, which I didn't even start dealing with yet, and Anthony who thinks that I have a drinking problem. "As bad as things are," I said, "it feels like it's just the beginning." Deedee grabbed my hands and said "Samantha, I'm sure you'll figure something out but if you need help, just say the word." "I know Deedee," I said as I let go of her hands for a much-needed hug.

"Well" she said with her forced heavy Spanish accent that always made me laugh "I don't know much about this school stuff, but I do have a nice bottle of wine that could help with your drinking problem and possibly this under the weather shit so how about it?" We got off the couch and headed for the kitchen for the wine.

By the time I got home that afternoon, I felt a little better. Not just because I had three glasses of wine but also because I now had a plan to solve some of my problems. I was so proud of myself that I wanted to share my good news so I picked up the phone and called Stanley for old time sake. "Samantha! How are you doing?" "I'm good Stanley; it feels like we haven't talked for so long." "Well, we really haven't" he said as a matter of fact "Are you looking for Anthony? He asked. As soon as the words came out of his mouth I realized that we never really talked about my dating his son. My heart started pounding as I realized that I might have made a mistake by calling, especially since I didn't know where he stood on the matter.

"Stanley, I'm sorry" I finally said, "I didn't want you to find out this way, it's just…" "Samantha" he cut in before I could finish "there's no need to apologize, both you and my son are adult enough to make your own decisions without my permission, wouldn't you say?" "I know…but" "Samantha…There's no but and no reason to be sorry" he interrupted again "are you kids happy?" "Yes we are," I answered as thoughts of Anthony and I being together ran through my mind. "Alright then why don't you tell me how things are going?"

I didn't know where to begin. I started telling him how badly I've screwed up with school and everything else but Stanley wanted details. So we talked about school, the club and the office, my going to jail and my new plan, which he thought was a good idea. The plan was that come Monday morning I was gonna go to Florida International University and fill out an application for their upcoming term as a transfer student where it would be a lot less of a financial burden. Then I was gonna drive to University of Miami and settle whatever mess I'd gotten myself into so I could get my transcripts. Stanley referred me to a lawyer whom he was gonna call to take care of my DUI situation and once that was done I was gonna quit the club, pay off whatever money I owe with what I had saved up, and work full time at the firm. I figure I could take night classes and work during the day. Although I didn't say it, my hopes were that my drinking and spending habits would subside once I was away form the life source of it all: "The Unicorn." As we were coming toward the end of our conversation, he asked me if Anthony knew about my job. The question caught me off guard and rendered me speechless for a second.

"No…" I said "I thought about telling him for a while but…I don't know Stanley, do you think I should?" "Samantha, that's something you'll have to decide" he said. "Have you?" I asked him. "That's not my place to tell him," he said. "Stanley…I really do love him, I guess I should of told him but I didn't want things to change between us, I thought I'd lose him if I did. I promise I'll tell him once this is all over." We were on the phone for almost two hours and as always it was nice to talk to Stanley and put things in perspective. He had a way of making you feel like there were better days ahead and Lord knows I could use some.

Friday seemed like the longest day in history. My body felt like it got run over by a truck. My nose was congested and running at the same time, everyone at the office seemed to be running on super charge mode and I was left trying to catch up. The only thing that kept me going was the fact that I was going to see Anthony that evening. After work, on my way to the car, I ran into Andrew whom I hadn't seen in a while. "Where you've been hiding?" he asked with his signature smile on his face. "I should be asking you that question, I've been here working and going to school, same old boring stuff," I said as he opened his arms to give me a hug. "So what are you up to? He asked. "Not much" I replied "I'm kind of feeling under the weather so I think I'm gonna head home and rest." "So much for me asking you out tonight" he said teasingly. "Where are you heading? I asked. "Running home to change then to the airport to pick up my brother." I don't know what he saw on my face but was now smiling from ear to ear as he said, "I think somebody has a crush on my brother…no wonder you won't let me take you out." "Bye Andrew," I said with an uncontrollable grin on my face as I hugged him goodbye.

On my way home I called Deedee to see if she had a confirmation on the estimate for the damage on her car. The estimation was still about $7,600 dollars. Deedee wanted to split the cost because she felt responsible for asking me to drive but the reality was I was behind the wheel she wasn't. After talking to her I drove to the bank and withdrew 8,000 dollars. I called Deedee back and asked her to stop by on her way to work. Anthony probably wouldn't come by until after 8:00 P.M. so I figured I had at least a couple of hours to get some rest. I stopped by a drug store grabbed some sinus and flu related medication, walked to the Italian deli next door for a chicken salad sub and by the time I got home, I was ready to collapse. Without the air on, I was so cold that I couldn't stop clattering my teeth long enough to eat. I dragged myself to the kitchen poured me a glass of Peppermint Schnapps to warm me up then changed out of my clothes which were now soaked with sweat. I woke up around 7:00 P.M. from the pounding on my door. "Where were you?" asked Deedee "we've been knocking for at least five minutes." "We?" I repeated to make sure I heard her right. She must have realized how bad I looked because she ignored my question, dropped her purse on the floor and dragged me to the couch. "Samantha, have you looked at yourself? You need to do something about this." "I'm okay Deedee I just need to…" before I could finish Danny walked in holding his phone. I turned around to look at Deedee. "Nick had to fly to Columbia with Rolly, my car's in the garage so Danny's giving me a ride to work" she said as if knowing I wanted an explanation. Danny came over and gave me his usual two-sided kiss and said "feels like you have a temperature; coming down with something?" "I think so," I said looking at him, as he got comfortable on the opposite couch. "Angel can I do anything or get anything for you?" Danny asked leaning forward. I really felt like shit but I didn't want Danny and Deedee to worry anymore than they had to. "Thanks guys but I'll be okay, I think I'm sweating it out. I should be fine after a good night's sleep." I grabbed the blanket from the side of the couch and wrapped myself up as I pulled and folded my legs Indian style. "Angel you gotta turn the air on, it's too stuffy in here" complained Danny as he got up as if looking for the thermometer. "I know, but I'm freezing." "Alright" he said looking at me sympathetically, "can I at least open the windows, you need some fresh air in here." "Go head Danny," Deedee ordered him then turned to address me "look I gotta get to work but I needed to talk to you about something." "Is it the car?" I asked "I got the mon…"

"No girl, I mean important stuff like business." I felt too sick to deal with important stuff but Deedee didn't look like she wanted to wait to tell me whatever it was. She turned to look at Danny who was still opening the living room windows and said "Danny you know more about it than I do why don't you tell her?" "Deedee," he stopped and sighed for a second then continued "you two are my homegirls and all but I told both you and Nick how I felt about you two getting involved so you do what you want but, I'm gonna go wait in the car. He bent over and kissed me on my cheeks and said, "Feel better mama." To Deedee he said, "Hurry up before you're late for work" as he walked out the door.

By now I was curious to know what they were talking about. Deedee moved next to me on the couch with excitement in her eyes. "Deedee you're making me nervous, what's up?" "Okay, okay…you know how you were talking about getting out of dancing?" "Yeah," I said trying to think of where she was going with this. "Well you've kind of made me think about things and how I'd like to do something with my life too…you know with me and Nick getting married…Maybe having a family someday…well, I wouldn't want to be where I am right now, you know." Usually Deedee's talk of the future would consist of what was coming up for the weekend or which one of our favorite stores was having a sale so it was really weird to hear her talking about serious stuff. "So, what are you thinking?" I asked wishing she'd just get to the point and tell me. "Well I think I've found a way for us to make some real money and start a new life…so hear this." The solution that Deedee had for us was a drug deal that involved Nick and Danny estimated to bring in at least 12 million dollars. "Deedee" I said cutting into her explanation, "I'm not trying to go to jail." "Just hear me out before you get all worked up…we're not gonna go to jail." I gave her this look that urged her to justify her statement. "Okay, remember Tim? That police officer that has been at the club with Rolly?" she asked hesitantly. "Uh uh." "He's in on the deal and thinks it's a smooth enough job. We could easily make at least a million for just a couple of hours." "And what would we have to do for that kind of money?" I asked pulling my blanket tighter. "Nick mentioned they might need a couple of unsuspected carriers so I thought we could help out and get a piece of the pie. I mean why should the boys have all the fun." "I don't know Deedee, I'd have to think about it…and what about Danny, what was he talking about?"

"Just ignore him, he claims that he doesn't want us to get involved in the deal but trust me he's only saying that because your name was mentioned, he's probably worrying that something might happened to you." "Yeah, yeah" I cut in sensing where she was going with this. "Nah I'm telling you Samantha he really likes you, I don't know why you guys don't just stop the bullshit and get together."

"Deedee don't start, don't you need to get your ass to work?" I said as I got off the couch and headed for my bedroom "and if you like him so much why don't you go out with him?" I continued. She followed me towards the door and said jokingly "maybe I should go out with him then the three of us could have ourselves a threesome." "You're so crazy," I said dropping myself on the bed as I threw a pillow at her. We were both laughing when we heard the door, knock.

"I'll see you later Deedee, it's probably Danny at the door, just lock up behind you." "Alright mama, I'll give you a call later to see how you're doing." With that she bent over to kiss me on the cheek and ran out the room yelling, "I'm coming." From my bed I heard the door open and Deedee's voice saying "Anthony! Long time no see."

For a brief moment I thought I was dreaming then I turned toward my clock which read 7:52 P.M. Oh no, I thought, I didn't realize it was so late, I should of called Anthony earlier because I really don't think I can leave my bed tonight. I was crawling out of the covers when I heard Danny saying, "it was nice seeing you again Anthony, Deedee we gotta go." "Likewise" Anthony answered then said goodbye to Danny and Deedee.

I was now in the living room, trying to look better than I felt as Anthony locked the door behind Danny and Deedee. "Hi baby" I said as I got near him. He turned around, pulled me in a bear hug and demanded "what are you doing out of bed?" "Making sure I wasn't dreaming," I said with a big grin on my face as I reached on my toes and laid a tender kiss on the side of his face. "That's the best you can do for a welcome kiss?" he asked pleadingly. "No, but I don't want to get you sick," I replied. "Well since the trial is over I think I can risk it," he said.

The news of his trial being over was as good as him being home for the weekend but before I could tell him how happy I was to hear that, he pulled me up and brought me to my toes for a long slow kiss. Andrew had warned Anthony of my being under the weather so he had cancelled our plans of going out and appointed himself as my caretaker. It was so nice to have him here with me. Although I felt bad ruining our celebration night, I soon realized that I was in no shape to be on my feet. With Anthony leading the way, I followed him back to my bedroom as he asked about how I was feeling, what was hurting, etc...I got in bed under the covers and Anthony climbed up next to me and started rubbing my forehead gently back and forth. "Do you have a thermometer?" he asked. "I don't, but I'm sure I've got a temperature. I've been freezing all afternoon and the air is not even on." I said. "Have you been able to keep food down?" he asked. As soon as he asked the question, I realized I never ate my sandwich from this afternoon. He must have read my mind, with disbelief in his eyes, he said, "sweetheart tell me you've had something to eat today." "I honestly forget; I stopped and bought a sandwich but I didn't have the appetite to eat it." He got off the bed to go find us some food but I knew there was nothing to eat in my fridge and my cupboards were nearly empty from last week. He came back in the room holding the half full bottle of Peppermint Schnapps. Before he could say a word I pushed myself up on my elbows and said, "I was freezing, I was trying to warm up." He placed the bottle on my dresser without a word about my comment then said, "Why don't we go to my place? We could pick something up on the way and I should have some stuff there that you could probably take."

We drove to Anthony's place and ordered some food on the way. By the time we got in, I was soaked with sweat and shivering with the chills. I was trying to act strong because Anthony wanted to take me to the hospital but ever since my father's death I've had this thing about hospitals so that's the last place I wanted to be. My temperature was 102 degrees so Anthony filled the tub with cold water hoping that the cold bath would help bring my temperature down. I felt so miserably cold that I thought I was gonna black out.

Anthony changed into some comfortable clothes and got our plates ready with the food that was delivered while I was in the tub. I laid in bed as Anthony spoon-fed me my lunch/dinner. He had finished his food, and went to his medicine cabinet when I realized that my food was making a round trip. I looked for the trash can and tried to call Anthony but the words came out with everything I'd manage to eat just a few minutes ago. The sound effect brought him running back to the room and one look at me in the middle of the mess he said "Baby I'm calling a doctor...come on we gotta get you cleaned up." My used to be clean clothes were peeled off of me, his dirty sheets were pulled off the bed and I was back where I least wanted to be, in the shower.

Anthony and I moved to his small guest room and once we were settled he called a friend of his, Robert Stuart, a doctor at Mercy Hospital. After telling him what was going on, he agreed to come by the next morning to look at me. "I'm sorry for messing up your night," I said. "Shush, shush, we're together aren't we? Just worry about getting better," he said as he placed butterfly kisses all over my face. Anthony and I stayed in bed with the TV on as he flipped through the channels. As I drifted off to sleep, I remember hearing him call his cleaning lady to ask her to come in the next day.

Not even an hour after I fell asleep I was awakening by my coughing and the clattering of my teeth from being so cold. Anthony got up and fixed me some chicken broth, which I managed to keep down successfully. He went back to his medicine cabinet to see if he had anything I could take but all he found was some Pepto-Bismol and a bottle of aspirin. We were gonna go with the aspirin but then I remembered that I'd gotten some stuff earlier from the drugstore. "Did you bring them with you? he asked. "They should be in my black leather tote bag, just look in there. I don't remember taking them out," I replied.

He went back to the master bedroom where we left my bags to look for the medicine and was gone for an uncomfortable while. I was lying there wondering whether he couldn't find my bag or if maybe I didn't have the medicine in there. "Are you okay?" I called out. He hesitated for a second before he answered and finally said that he was all right. When he finally came back with the medicine his mood seemed to have changed as if his thoughts were suddenly weighing him down. I took the two boxes from him, placed them on the bed, then reached for his hand and said "Why don't you get some rest before we both get sick. I'm sure you're exhausted from your trip?" He bent over and said, "I'm okay, I'm just worried about you." He placed a soft kiss on my lips then grabbed the two boxes from the bed to read the instructions.

I woke up the next morning finding Anthony with a cup of coffee in hand and a short medium built man next to my bed. The stethoscope around his neck indicated that he was the doctor that Anthony had called the night before. The voice coming from doctor forced me to focus my thoughts. "Looks like our patient is awake." My eyes focused on a head of curly black hair and a face that looked like he should be on a soccer field somewhere in Italy. "Don't worry," he said, "I've seen a patient or two before." My nose was so congested that I could hardly breathe but I managed to whisper, "Thanks for..." I couldn't finish my words because I started coughing. Anthony moved to the other side of the bed as Dr. Stewart went on with his consultation. "No need to thank me," he said "let's just get you better." He started asking questions about my symptoms and in between questions, instructions were being given to "take a deep breath, cough, open your mouth,..." After all equipment had been pulled out of his bag, used for his examination, and placed back, he diagnosed me as having a bad sinus infection and a case of pneumonia. I was placed on an antibiotic for a week and advised to come by his office in a week for a test because he also thought I might have asthma. I had no intention of going since I knew that the wheezing in my breathing and the chest pain was from all the smoke at my job but of course, I wasn't going to tell him that.

By Monday, I was starting to feel better but Anthony still decided to stay home with me. Tuesday, Andrew came by and was surprised to find me sleeping in Anthony's bed. I guess that's one way to confirm your brother's girlfriend.

By Thursday, I felt a lot stronger and was ready to go home. Dr. Stewart came by and told me I was in the clear but needed to keep taking my medicine. It was a beautiful day and Anthony and I wanted to go out and make up for the days we'd been cooped up inside. As much as we were in good spirits, I could tell that something was on Anthony's mind. I knew him so well that I didn't need word to know when something was wrong. That afternoon we were driving to the Grove for a sidewalk lunch when Deedee called me on the cell. It had been a few days since we spoke so I picked up the phone with the intention of letting her know I was okay and that I'd be calling her later. Our conversation was brief but before we hung up she reminded me to think about what we'd talked about.

"Can I ask you something?" Anthony's voice of concern that I'd been hearing for the past few days were turning into his interrogative lawyer's tone, which I was not accustomed to hearing. Something told me I wasn't going to like what he had to ask but what could I have said? I put on a big smile and told him to shoot, that smile was quickly wiped off my face when he asked me what Deedee and Danny did for a living. Not only could I not see where the question had come from but I also couldn't see where he was going with it. So as pleasantly as I could, I asked him why he wanted to know. Instead of answering my question, he posed another one of his own and asked the reason why Danny and Deedee were at my place this past Friday.

"Anthony, these people are my friends and I don't think I need a reason for them to come by my place. Besides why the interrogation all of a sudden?" I asked. "Because I feel like I'm in the dark sometimes," he answered with a deep sigh. "I just need some answers," he said running his hand through his hair. My mind was racing trying to find something to say but Anthony went on, "I'm not saying that your friends can't come to your house but I don't know what I'm supposed to think when I run into this guy Danny at your place and he's referring to you as Angel, then that same night I find 8,000 cash in your bag? We've been together for a while, you use your credit card for everything, why would you have all that money laying around?"

The minute he said 8,000, I remembered Deedee's money for the car. I can't believe I forgot to give it to her. Without thinking I heard myself asking, "What were you doing in my bag?"

"You sent me to your bag to get your medicine remember?" he said in disbelief. I'd clearly stuck my foot in my mouth so I opted to stop while I was ahead. It then occurred to me why he had taken so long to come back with the medicine that night at his place. He turned his head toward me with a look that spoke louder than words. The silence intensified by the seconds and finally he asked, "Are we gonna talk about this?"

The weight of my thoughts seemed to force the words down my throat. I really didn't know what to say without getting into things that I wasn't ready to talk about. "Anthony…" I finally managed to say, "I really understand how you feel but I'm really not up for this, can we talk about this some other time?" "Some other time when?" he demanded, his tone of voice triggered a nerve and I was trying real hard to keep my cool. I could understand his position but this was my first day from being sick and I wasn't ready for this shit so I launched back, "I still don't see the connection between my friends and our relationship so what's the big urgency?" Maybe there was and I just couldn't see it but Anthony didn't say anything so for now, his silence was gonna have to do.

We had a quiet lunch at a small café but neither one of us seemed hungry as we nibbled through our food. The drive back to my apartment was so tense you could cut it with a knife. It certainly wasn't the best way to show Anthony how grateful I was for taking such good care of me but I didn't expect having to deal with these questions either. I just wanted to be home alone so I could figure things out. "I'll call you later," I forced myself to say as we pulled in my parking lot. Without answering he got out of the car, walked around to my side to get my door as he normally did, grabbed my large bag and stood there waiting. I guess he wanted to be mad for a while.

When we reached my floor, I caught a glimpse of a large flower arrangement in front of a door down the hall. I took a deep breath and secretly hoped that it wasn't my door. The few proceeding steps proved me wrong. Anthony was behind me as I picked up the vase. The card read, "Get well soon, Love, Danny." I opened the door and placed the vase on my kitchen counter. Anthony was in the living room with my bag. "Thanks for all your help," I said joining him by the couch. "You're welcome," he replied after waiting for a second then said, "I think I'm gonna go…enjoy your flowers," he said pointing to the arrangement on the counter. I knew he'd read the card from the arrangement and with everything going on this was like adding insult to injury.

The few days that followed, Anthony and I barely talked to each other. Our nightly two hour conversations were now meaningless arguments or at best, minutes of forced conversations of how our day was, his days at the office, my health, etc. We both knew why but our hectic schedule seemed like a more likable excuse for the emotional distance between us.

My plan to get my life back on track was slowly unfolding. My transfer process from University of Miami to F.I.U. was almost complete and the only thing that was still somewhat of an issue were my finances. I paid off my car, some of my heavy credit card bills and the balance from U.M. Looking at what was left, I didn't see how I was going to survive without working at the club. Changes and adjustments had to be made and I just didn't know where to start. When I tried to figure things out, I was amazed to see how deep this business had sucked me into this current lifestyle that I now lived.

Weekend shopping spree at BAL Harbor, eating out or ordering in once or twice daily, my expensive drinking habits, not to mention trips here and there didn't come cheap. After all the payoffs, my bank account balance was $1,700. I still had my rent, utilities, school tuition and books for the upcoming fall semester. I guess the $19,000 payoff on my car was not such a good idea after all. I just didn't wanna have a 12% interest monthly bill to worry about. As much as I didn't want to, it seems like I was gonna have to do a week or so at the club to build some cushion until I started full-time at the office.

One afternoon I got a call from Deedee asking me to come by if I had a chance. I hadn't seen her since that Friday when she and Danny came by, so I decided to go by after leaving the office. I figured I'd get a chance to give her the money for the car repair and catch up on Deedee's drama. The whole crew was at her place: Nick, Danny, Tim the cop, and Jerry who I'd seen a few times at Nick's. They were in the living room drinking and smoking and in the middle of a heated conversation about football. I thought of saying something to Danny about the flower arrangement but decided against it since as usual I didn't know whether to thank him or yell at him. After a quick hello to the guys, Deedee and I made our way to her bedroom where she told me that I needed to give her an answer about the deal. I'd been toying with the idea for the past few days but the reality was I didn't know enough about the deal to make a sound decision. She told me that she'd have Nick explain the plan to me whenever they were done fucking around with their football nonsense. She fixed us two glasses of Long Island Ice Tea and proceeded to the balcony. As the cold drink refreshed us from the hot and humid Florida afternoon, we talked about business at the club, the girls that either left or just started, my customers who'd been asking about me and of course our favorite topic, the plans for Deedee's wedding.

My intended quick-pass-by visit had turned into a couple of hours. Three Long Island Ice Teas Later, Jerry and Tim were gone and Nick was able to give me some detail about the deal. Danny wasn't as talkative as he usually was; there were no jokes, and no smart-ass remarks when I'd ask Nick a question...nothing. He just sat on the couch smoking in between sips from his glass. After talking to Nick and promising to let him know by the end of the week, I told Deedee I'd call her the next day and kissed everybody goodbye.

I was about to get in the elevator when I spotted Danny down the hallway. "I'll walk you to your car" he yelled across the hall. "Are you asking or telling me?" I asked when he finally reached me. Without answering me, he stepped halfway into the elevator, which had just opened, leaving one leg out to prevent the door from closing. I got in the elevator and before I could reach the lobby buttons, Danny's finger beat me to it.

"Why didn't you ever tell me that your name was Samantha?" he asked as we started to go down. "Why do you care?" I asked. He spared me a glance and tapped his pockets for his lighter to light the cigarette he was holding in his hand. "You can't smoke in the elevator..." I said returning his glance then asked, "How did you find out?" He waited a second then said "I was talking to your old man the other day. I mentioned your name or what I thought was your name and I got some bad vibes from our conversation. I mentioned it to Deedee and she told me that your old man didn't know about your job or your name. Did he say anything?" Thoughts of Anthony and everything going on between us ran through my head but I didn't see the point of filling Danny in. "Does it really matter?" I asked. "Look," he said in his smooth talking style, "I guess I'm trying to say I'm sorry. As much as I'd like a chance with you, I don't want you to think that I'd purposely mess things up for you." "Is that why you left the flowers at my door?" I asked.

We were now approaching my car he stopped dead in his tracks and said, "You're fucking welcome." I turned around to face him and his eyes were filled with anger. "The flowers for your information got there before I found out about your name. Your home girl's the one who talked me into leaving them. Trust me I've been kicking myself for days for listening to Deedee so don't flatter yourself." I stood there speechless, feeling the long island ice tea kicking in. Danny filled in the distance between us with a few lazy steps and said, "You have a way of bringing the fool out of me…" "Dan…" "Nah, nah…it's my own fucking fault," he said with a sinister laugh. He turned and walked away leaving me frozen in place. I guess I was on a roll at getting all the men in my life upset.

Things were starting to smooth out between Anthony and me although we both knew that something still needed to be worked out. I was slowly opening up to him, talking about my childhood, and my dad. He was being very patient and understanding. We talked about my friendship with Danny and reassured him that he had nothing to worry about because I had no intention of doing anything to jeopardize our relationship. I told him about the car accident, leaving out the prison and the DUI part, which explained why I had 8,000.00 that night in my purse.

Since I was trying to lead the straight life I decided not to go in on the deal with Deedee. Although the money was tempting, the idea of ending up in jail or losing Anthony if something went wrong seemed too high of a price to pay. So I went back to the club and figured I'd work a few weeks for some cushion money and by then, Stanley would be back in town and I'd be starting full time at the office.

Anthony had been working long hours in the office and up late into the night trying to catch up from being gone so long. On the days that I worked at the office, if we didn't see each other during lunch or after work, we'd meet at his place or he'd come by my apartment before he went back to work. With his hectic schedule, which I was banking on lasting for at least a few weeks, it was easy for me to go back to the club without him knowing.

Upon my return to the Unicorn, I told Larry that I was planning on quitting in the next couple of weeks. He looked at me, laughed, and then said, "That's what they all say!" He was right, except unlike these other girls, I wasn't just saying these words, I meant every bit of them. That night, I tried as hard as I could to stay away from the bar. Since Deedee wasn't working, it didn't seem so hard, but then some of my customers came by and wanted to celebrate my being back. I was on my fourth shot of Tequila and a few bottles of Champagne before I remembered to water down my drinks with apple cider.

CHAPTER 12

Tim got a hold of some coke from a couple of busts that were made a while back with a market value of 12 million dollars. The coke was supposed to be split between three major buyers. One of the buyers was Rolly's client and the other two were clients of Nick and Tim. Danny, who seemed to be the coordinator of the group, arranged for a sampling party once the buyers were confirmed and checked out.

A couple of weeks before the party, Deedee's new lawyer tracked Louis down and delivered the divorce papers. Unlike the previous time, Deedee didn't seem as stressed as she usually was whenever she had to deal with Louis. She'd gotten to the point where she didn't even care whether he signed the divorce papers or not because once this deal was over, her and Nick were packing up and moving to Belize.

Deedee

A few days after the papers were delivered to Louis, Nick and I, along with his crew went to "Calle Ocho," a Spanish festival in Hialeah. We were standing around, enjoying the music from the band on stage, talking, and smoking our cigars, when the boys stepped away for a refill on beer. I was dancing by the stage waiting for the boys to come back when I felt someone grab my ass. I turned around, thinking it was Nick, only to find Pedro, one of Louis compadres and Louis on the side by one of the vendors standing by with a handful of his friends looking and laughing at us like it was funny. I pushed Pedro away and told him to back off hoping that Nick didn't see anything. Every ounce in my body told me to go for a kick right up his cajones but I restrained myself knowing that a mixture of Louis and Nick in the same place was a sure recipe for trouble. As the idiot tried to come back and grab me in hope of putting on a show for his friends, I threw my beer in his face and stepped out of his reach hoping that he'd just go away.

"You stinking hoe" he said as he tried to reach for me again but this time his attempt was welcomed by Jerry, one of Nick's friends who's always looking for a good fight, with a fist right up his face. Before I knew what was going on, Pedro was on the floor trying to fight off Jerry. Louis' gang jumped on Jerry and, of course, Nick and the whole crew joined in to help Jerry. Louis and his crew were apprehended, charged, taken in. Because Tim (the K-9 officer on Nick's crew) got hit a few times, the were also charged with assaulting an officer.

The Friday after they got out, Louis showed up at the club, claiming that he wanted to talk to Deedee. The bouncer, like most of us at the club, knew Louis or had heard of him so everyone was kind of waiting for something to happen but Louis was quite calm. He talked to Deedee for a while until it was time for her to go on stage. He watched her performance and then vanished. That night as Deedee and I drove home, she told me about her conversation with Louis. In reality he did most of the talking; asking Deedee for another chance, telling her that he still loved her, asking why she wanted the divorce. Deedee explained to him the fact that she was in love with Nick and that there was no chance of them ever getting back together. Louis talked about the good times they'd shared and Deedee thought that he was finally letting go.

Saturday night, Deedee went to Nick's to spend the night and Sunday afternoon she unlocked her car door getting ready to come home and found a large manila envelop on her seat. She freaked out and had Nick look inside. Surprisingly, it was a copy of her divorce papers, all shredded up with a copy of her and Louis' marriage certificate. She just couldn't believe it. She started panicking at the thought that Louis had followed her to Nick's and broke into her car without setting off the alarm.

From that time on, Deedee kept saying that she felt like someone was following her but Nick swore she was just losing her mind. With the sampling party coming up and trying to set things up in Belize, Nick didn't want to be bothered with anything. Deedee was becoming so paranoid that she was now afraid even of her own shadow so as if I could do anything, I became Deedee's bodyguard. Every time she wanted to go somewhere, she'd call me to go along with her. Sometimes she'd call me in the middle of the night and beg me to come over because she thought she'd heard something. On the nights when Nick or myself wasn't around, Deedee would drive to South Beach, go clubbing until it was closing time, and then end up in somebody's bed for the night. In Deedee's world, sex was the answer to everything so she figured she was dealing with the situation the best way she knew how. I just wish that her method of dealing with her issues didn't cause me so much stress.

It was my last week back at the club. Two more days to go and I was counting the hours when I would kiss Unicorn goodbye forever. That Wednesday at the office after work, the office manager came and asks me if I could swing by the office tomorrow for the surprise birthday lunch they were having for Andrew.

Andrew's office was filled with balloons and gifts from his female fan club. Trudy, the office manager, baked a cake and ordered some snacks. Around 1:00 P.M., when most of the crew from our floor was back from court or other engagements, Trudy tricked Andrew into one of the conference rooms where everybody was waiting and ready to yell "SURPRISE!!!"

Well those are the kind of things that happened when you worked with someone like Trudy who had watched this young man grow up into the man that he is today. Trudy never missed a chance to tell the story of the first time she met Andrew and Anthony at 7 and 4 years old. She'd been with the firm for twenty years, first in England, than in the States after her husband died and where she could be close to her daughter.

Andrew, whether surprised or not, acted the part and went around thanking everybody. Anthony, after wishing his brother a Happy Birthday, joined me in the corner where I stood letting Andrew enjoy his spotlight. Anthony was telling me how tired he was when Donald came by and asked him about joining them tonight for a birthday celebration for Andrew. Anthony told him that he'd have to take a rain check and pass since he had but a few days to finish the contract he'd been working on.

"Do you really have to work so hard?" I asked feeling his pain. "Unfortunately for now, yes," he confirmed. "Don't worry things should be back to normal by next week." Those were the moments I wished I could make everybody disappear and kiss him to make things better, but except for Andrew, and I suspected Donald, no one at the office knew about me and Anthony. That explains why some of the girls at the office would constantly try to make passes at him or fantasized out loud about him in front of me in the lunchroom. As far as the office staff was concerned, I was a friend of the Wellington family who happened to be doing her internship at the firm.

Anthony and I were walking around the room making small talk with some of the staff as we enjoyed the refreshments and desserts, all the while wishing we could be alone. Somehow we both ended up by the door and as if reading each other's mind, I slipped out and made a quiet run for his office. As Anthony followed, we were like two kids playing hide-and-go-seek, peeping through the blinds making sure that no one else followed. Without a word, Anthony locked his door. Holding my hand, he led us into his changing room where he kept a few suits in case he ever had to change without going home. I found his lips, soft and ready. I lowered myself to undo his tie and unbutton his shirt with every intention to follow up on the kiss. He unzipped the back of my dress and let if fall to the floor. We found our way to the couch, where he brought his lips to mine, and got on top of me to keep me in place. His mood went from tired to possessive as he slew me with every stroke of caress. I hooked my legs around his, he tucked his hand under my hips and lifted me. I looked into his eyes and understood that he needed me. We soon fell into this rhythmic motion making sure we didn't make a sound. We melted into one complete being.

"We should go back," I whispered, "they might notice that we're gone." "Let them," he said as he nibbled on one of my ears. We sat quietly in each other's arms as our heart rate slowed to the beat of the oversized clock on the wall. I closed my eyes for a second and slowly forced myself out of his arms, "You gotta get back to work," I said, retrieving my clothes from the floor while thinking "too bad we couldn't stay here forever."

I went into the small bathroom behind the closet to freshen up and Anthony followed with his clothes.

"If I get this contract done by Friday, you think I could be lucky enough to have you for a weekend get-away?" he asked softly as he tried to stop me from getting my clothes on. The tenderness in his eyes softens my heart as if I was falling in love all over again. "We'll see," I teased him as I pushed him out the door.

Once we were both freshened up and dressed, I told Anthony I had to go. He was gonna stay and work on his contract and possibly go to the gym. I talked him into letting me leave alone in case I ran into anyone from the office.

There was a private elevator toward the end of the hall that was rarely used due to its inconvenient location. Anthony found the key and gave it to me to use to eliminate the possibility of running into anyone.

For a Thursday night, the club was packed with customers from the bar all the way to the Champagne Room. Deedee and I were sitting at the bar when she put her glass down and exclaimed "I can't believe we're getting the fuck out of here!" "We? Since when did "we" make that decision?" I asked pointing at her. "You didn't think you were leaving without me did you?" I shook my head with a smile realizing how much we've rubbed off on each other over the years.

"Are you for real?" I asked with a smile on my face. "Hell yeah," she confirmed, "I'm looking at close to 1.5 million with this deal, you know it's not too late to join," she whispered. "Thanks but no thanks," I laughed.

It was time for Deedee to go on stage. We raised our shot glass filled with Tequila for a toast before Deedee went up for her performance. The night was going smoothly. Deedee and I barely had time to visit the dressing room; we were either on stage, talking to a customer or doing a table dance. Of course, a busy night meant heavy drinking although for some reason that night I wasn't feeling the effect as much as I normally did.

It was 11:00 P.M. and one of my customers whom I hadn't seen in a while showed up in the mood to party. After telling him that Deedee and me were quitting, he decided to go on a private dance spree with the two of us. We must have been on our 6th or 7th song when we heard some cheers coming from the bar. I was trying to figure out what was going on and concluded it to be some of the girls or customers with too much alcohol in their system.

The DJ came on announcing that I was on deck for the next performance. As the song finished I got my outfit back on and told my customer I had to go on stage. He told me he was gonna be at the bar to watch my performance. I walked to the stage to the rhythm of "More Human Than Human" by White Zombie and five seconds into my performance I grabbed the brass poll ready to do one of my famous swings, when I spotted Andrew and Donald by the large bar with two girls performing a table dance. They must have spotted me at the same time because at that instant Donald stood up stuck his two index fingers in his mouth, whistled as loud as he could then yelled "go Samantha!" As if that wasn't bad enough, the situation worsened when the men's bathroom door opened and out came Anthony. My heart froze. Anthony stood still staring at me with a look of disgust that cut straight through my heart without a word. I ran off the stage hoping that this was all a bad dream. He was now back at his table where both Andrew and Donald were standing with confusion on their faces. The DJ was on the microphone calling me to go back on stage but with Anthony standing there I could only be Samantha, Angel seemed like somebody else to me. I stood in front of Anthony feeling as nude as I've ever been. "Anthony," I called pleadingly as he walked away.

Without even looking at me, he told Andrew and Donald that he was leaving. They both followed him out the door leaving me standing by the two girls who were previously entertaining them. Forgetting that I was half naked, I ran out the door and cut in front of Andrew and Donald to their car where Anthony was standing by the passenger door. "I'm sorry," I said "I was gonna tell you…" "Really?" he asked with sarcasm and anger in his voice. "And just when was that? When it was convenient for you? Looks like I've saved you the trouble."

Every inch of his body reflected his anger; the outline of the veins from his arms to his neck indicated the rapid flow of blood that deepened his skin tone. At first I was at a loss for words hoping that the tightness in my throat would not unleash the tears that were ready to flow. Anthony didn't want to hear anything out of my mouth; he claimed that I played him for a fool, that everything was a game to me. What few words came out of my mouth in an attempt to defend myself, he didn't want to hear it. In the middle of it all, Deedee came outside and covered me up with a jacket then grabbed my hand telling me to come back in. Andrew started the car and Anthony got in the passenger seat.

The tears flowing down my face rendered me blind as Deedee pulled me into the dressing room. Some of the girls were coming in to find out what was going on. I lowered myself to the ground and sank my head down, hugging my knees as tight as I could as if I was trying to hold everything in my world trying to put things back together.

"She's fine," I heard Deedee say, "nosy ass bitches" she mumbled under her breath as soon as the girls were out of the dressing room. "Dee…dee," I erupted into tears "what am I gonna do?" She was on the floor in front of me rubbing my back and wiping the tears off my face. "Come on mama, let's get outta here." She grabbed my clothes from my locker, helped me out of my outfit and into my clothes then told me to wait. I sat in the dressing room alone crying and thinking of how I'd just lost the best thing in my life.

Deedee came back with two Long Island Ice Teas and told me that she'd spoken to Larry and told him that we were leaving.

We drove straight to Deedee's place because she thought I might do something stupid if I was left alone. By the time we got to her place it started to rain. Deedee unlocked the door to let me in. Without the lights on I went into her fridge and pulled out two beers. The living room was lit just enough to see from the reflection of the outside lights coming through the balcony glass door. Deedee followed me into the kitchen. Leaving the lights off, she grabbed her bottle opener, removed the beer caps and quietly we sat in the dark watching the rainfall. "Should I call him?" I asked through silent tears. "I don't think that's a good idea," Deedee answered in between gulps, "he might need some time to cool off." Eventually Deedee went to bed but I stayed up crying and drinking as I watched the rain drum against the balcony's glass door.

By Sunday I still hadn't heard from Anthony. Periodically I tried calling but he never answered. Deedee kept telling me to just let it go but I couldn't. It's like asking me to stop breathing; I couldn't just stop loving him or forget about him.

There's no way I could go back to the firm and face those guys so by late Sunday night, I realized I was gonna have to call Stanley and let him know that I wasn't planning on going back to the firm. I thought of telling him about what happened but I didn't want him to feel stuck in the middle since this was between me and his son. Finally I phoned Stanley and left a message at his office. My message was short without details just thanking him for his continuous support, that I had some things going on that needed to be resolved and would not be returning to the firm. I told him not to worry that I was fine and promised to call him soon.

As the days went by the pain got worse. Not just because Anthony never attempted to call or see me but also because I didn't know whether we were through or if he was just mad for the time being. When I finally went home, I'd sit by the phone looking through our pictures hoping he'd call but the only calls I got were usually from Larry trying to get me to come back to work, Danny to check on me, Deedee checking on me or freaking out because she thought she either heard something or someone following or watching her. On occasions I'd drive over wherever she was which was usually at a club and spend the night with her just so she'd feel better but in between those few occasions most of my nights would end up with me sobbing myself to sleep.

I'd sometimes call Deedee to see if she wanted to come over just to take my mind off of things but with Nick and the boys so engulfed in their deals, Deedee was spending more time at the clubs on South Beach which most of the time ended up with her waking up in some stranger's bed. I tried to tell her how much she was adding to my stress by having me worry whether or not I was gonna see her on the news one of these days but having fun took precedence over safety when it came to Deedee, especially when she saw her actions as therapeutic. I just hope Nick never finds out because then we wouldn't have to worry about the weirdoes or Louis putting her on the news because Nick would for sure take care of that.

A week and a half went by and my mind was debating whether to find a way to see him or get over him. Deedee was pushing for the latter but for someone who was picking up men and women at the bars then claiming she was in love with her fiancé, I didn't think she was in a position to understand how I felt about Anthony.

One afternoon while hanging out with Deedee, my cell phone rung. Nonchalantly, I picked up and nearly died when I heard Anthony's voice on the other end. I signaled Deedee to shut up and she immediately understood who it was. He asked me how I was and wanted to know if he could see me later that night. The sound of his voice instantly brought tears to my eyes. Having no intension of letting him know how broken I was, I gathered my strength and told him I'd be home around 8:00 P.M. As my heart screamed out loud "I love you," I simply said, "I guess I'll see you later?"

"Yeah...later" he responded.

Both lines were now dead but I could still hear his voice in my head as I dreaded what I knew would be our last meeting. Deedee moved next to me and asked if I wanted her to stay with me for support but I had to do this alone. Besides she was helping the boys out with some stuff relating to the deal so she promised to call when she was done.

Right before 8:00 P.M. the phone rang and I automatically thought it'd be Anthony telling me that he was running late or couldn't make it but rather it was some girl claiming to be Danny's girlfriend wanting to know why my number was on speed dial on her boyfriend's cell phone; the stupid things that women do sometimes. I bet you Danny was probably at one of his bimbo's place getting laid and this airhead was calling me, who had no interest in her man. She tried to ask me questions but with my own issues in mind I kept telling her that she needed to talk to Danny. My refusing to play into her hands got her even more upset so finally I just hung up. A few minutes later Anthony knocked on my door.

As I let him in, the awkwardness of not knowing whether to hug, kiss or shake hands tensed up the air. As if on queue, we both said hi and tried to think of the next thing to say. My heart was galloping with uncertainty, I moved towards the couch in case he wanted to sit but he followed and stayed standing. As he started to talk, my eyes searched for a focus point in hope that not looking into his eyes would not trigger my tears. Unable to withstand the silence I blurted, "I am so sorry Anthony, I didn't mean to hurt..." "Look Samantha," he cut in "this is very hard for me..." he paused for a moment breathing deep into the silence then calmly said "I thought I'd be able to talk to you, I guess part of me wanted to see you but obviously this is harder than I thought it'd be." He was now pacing back and forth by the couch. "I need some time to get my thoughts together and figure things out, right now I don't think

I can deal with this…with us. I'm…" "Anthony, what are you saying?" "I don't know, I'm so numb I don't' even know how or what I'm supposed to feel," "You hurt me," he said slowly looking into my eyes. "I need to figure some things out." "Anthony," I called out but he was already gone.

I watched him walk out my door knowing well that he wouldn't be back. I didn't know whether to feel sorry or hate myself. As much as I was tired of crying, my tears, which lately had been on standby started flowing quietly, down my face. I went around the apartment turning off all the lights and then crawled into bed with a bottle of Jack Daniel's and a couple of beers. The outside light poured through the side bedroom window making geometrical shapes with the shadow of the blinds. I sat against my headboard staring into the night. The phone rang and noises from the cars coming or leaving echoed from the parking lot. Everything stood still as the darkness took me back to the starless, homeless nights in dad's old pickup truck. The thought of my dad watching me from above made it even worse knowing how disappointed he must be with how I've screwed up my life. I ventured down memory lane as I emptied the bottle.

I woke up on the floor with the warmth of the sun on my face wondering where I was. A few glances at the familiar fixtures and the empty bottle next to me brought me back to the present. I instinctively reached for a half empty bottle but my bad aim knocked one of the bottles over spilling the leftover beer. I pushed myself off the floor and the oh-so familiar hangover headache hit me like a brick. I laid back on the floor for what seemed an eternity before I finally decided to jump into the shower.

I spent three days in the house without answering the phone or turning on the lights. I was barely eating and my alcohol supply was quickly depleting. Friday night, I crashed out on my bed when I thought I heard someone at my door. I'm not sure whether I drifted off to sleep or blacked out but the next thing I knew, Deedee was standing over me trying to wake me up as she pulled the blanket that covered my face. "Hey girl, what are you doing here?" I hoarsely asked. She poised for a second taking in a deep breath then switched to the psycho Latino bitch that she could be. "What am I doing here?" she repeated, "checking on your ass; what the hell you think you're doing getting me scared like that?" I was still trying to snap out of it trying to figure out how she got in. Before I could even say a word, she started yelling again. "Why didn't you answer you phone? I thought something happened to you."

I was hoping she'd stop yelling. I grabbed my head hoping to subdue my headache, which had been my loyal companion for the past few days. My reaction stopped Deedee in mid-sentence who immediately lowered herself to the bed and with concern in her voice asked me if I was okay. "Yeah," I answered, "I just need you to stop yelling before my head explodes." "I'll stop yelling," she said "I was so worried," she continued, "I thought something happened or Anthony did something to you. I was getting ready to have the boys go down to his office and have a talk with him if I didn't get a hold of you tonight." "Dee, I'm sorry," I lazily said, "I just didn't wanna face anybody." "So it's over between you guys?" she asked. I looked at her and just nodded my head. "Well you know you can't stay locked up in here forever," she said. Then with her natural flare back in her voice, she continued, "Well fuck Anthony, let's get this place cleaned up and we gotta get you cleaned up too cause you look like shit."

I exhaled with an exhausted smile at Deedee being herself. I knew I looked like shit and I felt like shit too. She started picking up the trail of mess that was all over the place: bags of open potato chips and empty wine bottles. As I made my way to the bathroom, I asked her how she got in; she told me that the building manager let her in after flirting and sharing a joint with him. So much for security, I thought.

By the time we were done cleaning up, we were both starving so Deedee suggested that we go out to eat. I really didn't feel like going anywhere I just wanted to be in bed and be left alone but Deedee kept telling me how much I needed some fresh air. We went downstairs and instinctively I started to look around for Deedee's BMW because riding in my Mustang was never an option when the Beamer was there. But it was nowhere to be found so I asked her where her car was. "I took a cab here," she answered. Turning to look at her I asked "Is something wrong with the Beamer?" "Oh no," she answered passively, "this Louis thing is just getting out of hand and I didn't want him to follow me here so I took a cab." "I thought this Louis thing was over," I asked. "I wish," she replied, "I swear he's just waiting to do something." She paused. "I saw him twice last week on South Beach when I was leaving a club." "Are you sure it was him?" I asked. "Samantha I was married to the man, trust me that was Louis. Besides, the last time, he made it a point for me to see him. I was about to get in my car when I saw him and thank God a couple of the guys from the club came up to talk to me so I had one of them ride with me because I knew he was gonna follow me. God only knows what he was gonna do."

We made our way to my car and I handed Deedee the keys. "Are you gonna tell Nick about this?" I asked. "Girl, you've been cooped up in that apartment way too long. You know Nick doesn't know that I'm out clubbing when he's gone. I just gotta wait a couple of weeks before the last deal with the boys go through then I'll be gone to Belize and he can shove the divorce up his ass!" For a moment we were both quiet. I guess we both had things on our mind. At least I didn't have a psycho stalking me.

I had to admit that after a decent meal and some fresh air, I felt a whole lot better. We went back to my apartment and since Deedee was looking for a reason not to go home these days and had no plans of her own, I asked her if she wanted to spend the night. I knew I could use the company besides it'd be like old time, like when I used to live at her place. As soon as we walked in she started looking for my phone. For some reason I couldn't remember what I did with my portable phone so I asked her why she couldn't use her cell phone. "I gotta cover my tracks girl. I've been telling Nick that I've been hanging with you when he's gone so if I call from your place, your number will show on his phone and it'll be like evidence you know." I shook my head at her and jokingly said, "Girl it's not enough that you're a whore you gotta think like one too?" "I tried to be the best at what I do," she replied with a smile.

The night ended up with both of us in the living room, drinking and Deedee trying to teach me how to look cool with a cigarette. The TV was on but we were barely watching it because we were too busy talking nonsense about Anthony, what I was gonna do, the deal with the boys, and an upcoming party that Deedee and Nick were planning for next week that she wanted me to help her with. I asked her what the party was for and she told me it was an engagement/celebration for the deals and a goodbye party all in one although nobody knew they were leaving for good. The party was next week Saturday, five days before the last deal. The next day or so after the deal, they were planning on going to Belize for their wedding and then to Mexico for good. "You should join in the last deal and come with us Samantha. This way you could be my maid of honor," suggested Deedee. "What am I gonna do in Mexico?" I asked. "Same thing you're doing here, nothing except you'd be my maid-of-honor doing nothing with money in the bank." She waited then continued, "You're really all I got for family down here and you're my best friend...we've been through so much together, I just don't wanna lose you and I don't know when or if we'll ever come back to the States...besides with Anthony gone I don't know what would be keeping you down here."

"What about school?" I asked her. "I'm sure there are schools in Mexico but with all the money you're gonna have, what the hell you need school for?" As I thought about it, I had to admit Deedee was right. I really didn't have a reason to be here. I came to Florida for one thing, "to go to school" and I've done a great job at fucking that up. It was sad to say but Deedee was the closest thing I had to a family and if she left…"You know Danny might be coming with us," Deedee said bringing me out of my thoughts. "What is that supposed to mean?" I asked, "and speaking of Danny, you know one of his girlfriends has been calling here cursing me out?" She started laughing then said, "Girl don't even sweat it, the bitch has been calling my house too. I had to tell Danny to put her in check before I did it for him." Laughing out loud I said, "I guess I can't miss your wedding hey?" Realizing the implication of my words she started screaming with excitement.

The days that followed, Deedee and I spent most of the days planning the party and getting trained by Danny for the upcoming deal. We must have driven the different routes for the delivery a hundred times and played out every possible problem that could possibly arise. One thing I had to admit was these boys knew their craft. At night we'd usually end up on South Beach where some lucky girl or guy would end up taking Deedee home for the night. Those nights, on my way home, I'd ponder at the reality of how little Deedee understood the concept of marriage but again Nick didn't understand that a woman needed more than just money to make her happy. Who knows? Maybe they were a perfect match for each other. This hectic schedule of dealing with Deedee's wedding and the party gave me something other than the loss of Anthony to focus on.

On Thursday and Friday, Deedee and I spent all day doing last minute shopping for the party. By 6:00 P.M. Saturday, Nick's house was alive with loud music, smoke, alcohol, the best that Cuban cuisine had to offer, and half-naked people running around in their swimsuits. Everyone seemed to be having a good time. Clearly the work Deedee and I had placed into the planning paid off. Most of the guests were under the impression that they were celebrating Nick and Deedee's engagement party but in all honesty, Nick never needed a reason to throw a bash because most people willingly came for the free buzz, free food, drugs and for many, a free piece of ass. This was not to say that their engagement wasn't worth celebrating. But this party was more of a celebration for the success of the first part of the deal. Most of the money was now safe in some offshore bank and we were all counting the days to the last deal.

CHAPTER 13

The sun had just vanished behind the horizon on Tuesday afternoon as I headed east toward our meeting place for the last deal. My heart was beating so fast; I couldn't believe I was really going through with this. I knew this was the last phase of the deal and it was a first and last for me. Nevertheless, I was nervous. It was a big risk but I had a lot to gain. I had to keep telling myself that everything would go well because after all, these boys were no amateurs; they were good at what they did.

When I got to the warehouse off of Coral Way, one of the locations where we'd done some of our training, everybody was already there. Their cars were pulled inside the building with all the windows closed. A couple of lights were on and everybody was sitting calmly smoking and drinking beers nothing hard because we had to be able to think straight. We had two deals going on. Danny and Al (Nick's brother) were closing a deal near Las Olas with one of their regular buyers. The second deal was in The Grove with a crew from Russia that was to be executed by Nick, Deedee, Jerry and myself. We were sitting around buying time. Deedee and I were talking about the future and she was teasing me about having to learn Spanish when we got to Mexico and before we knew it, it was time for action. Danny was scheduled to leave first and as he was leaving, he hugged me and told me I'd be fine and wished me luck. I opened my mouth to say the same but he read my mind and said "Don't need it, I got my gun." He winked his eye, got in the rental car and drove away. Minutes later, Nick checked his watch and told us it was time to go. We got into Nick's car drove down Ludland Road to another warehouse where Tim (the K9 officer) was waiting for us with a limo and a rental car. Tim and Jerry went in the back to talk for a brief minute then came back dressed like chauffeurs with a jacket, hat, and two radios similar to the one I'd used during training. I got in the rental car and was the first to leave to secure our spot in the block directly across the building where the limo was going. The meeting was scheduled for 10:00 P.M. at a high-end three-story vacation condo rental in a secluded area away from the Coco Walk crowd.

The streets were barely lit when the limo pulled up to the place. Sitting across the block in the car, I watched Jerry get out of the limo and get the door for Nick and Deedee who was sporting one of those long skinny cigarettes you normally see on TV. Jerry got the two suitcases out and followed Nick and Deedee into the building. A smile came to my face as I watched Deedee spiced things up with her walk, the cigarette, and the hand gestures. Minutes later, Jerry was back in the limo waiting.

Nick and Deedee were to return in 15 minutes with a done deal with half of the money wired to an account and the other half in hand. They would drive around to meet me and I was to drive them away where Danny and Al would be waiting. Jerry and I had a time limit on how long we were supposed to wait before he would go in and I'd have to drive around to pick them up.

The longest eight minutes of my life went by; Jerry called in to see if I was okay. I was staying calm but starting to sweat. Jerry was watching the surrounding areas and I was focused on the third floor penthouse where the deal was taking place. Other than the third floor the building was supposed to be empty and the third floor was purposely chosen because it was the floor with the penthouse where the elevator opened directly into the living room. The elevators in the first and second floor were in the hallways overlooking the street with tall cathedral windows. I placed the radio down, looked up and noticed a man all in black standing in front of the elevator. I picked up the binoculars to look and to my disbelief it was Louis.

"Fuck," I thought out loud. I grabbed the radio and told Jerry that someone was in the building waiting for the elevator on the second floor that looked like Louis. "Get ready just in case," he said and before I could respond he was out of the car racing up the stairs. I'm not sure who made it up there first but next thing I heard was the sound of gunshots coming from the third floor. All of a sudden it seems like it got real dark through the window. I watched the silhouettes of bodies moving and being thrown all over the place. A chorus of shots echoed into the night each holding on to their sound. Lord knows I wasn't trained for this. I backed out of my spot and drove around to the front of the building, all the while wondering what I should do. As I pulled up Nick came out covered with blood with Deedee and a suitcase in his arm. I pushed open the back door and with swiftness and great effort Nick threw Deedee in and slid next to her. "Holy shit Deedee's been shot," I screamed. "Deedee, Deedee, oh shit, oh shit, Nick she's not answering...we gotta get her to a doctor."

I started to go but Nick said "Jerry's coming." The words came out with a gush of blood out of his chest. "Oh fuck, you've been shot too," I exclaimed. A couple more shots went off then Jerry came out running toward the car with a black suitcase. Just as he reach the car a ray of bullets was let into his body and the car. I ducked down as if that was gonna do anything and secretly considered myself dead. Jerry's head and the suitcase fell right into the passenger window, I tried to open the door but his body was too heavy. "I ain't gonna make it, just go," he whispered, "Give me your gun." As tears flowed down my face I reached for the pistol under the seat and gave it to him. "Drive," Nick yelled holding on to his chest. The shots started again and the car's back window shattered. I stepped on the gas as I watched Jerry with bullet holes all over his body trying to shoot away with his last breath. "What if he's not dead?" I asked trying not to sound like I was crying. "Just get the fuck out of here," he replied in between his teeth.

I quickly looked back at Deedee and she was covered with Nick's jacket, blood all over and her eyes barely moving. I looked outside and realized that my right side mirror was gone. I finally got on the main street. I didn't know if I was being followed and I'm freaking out that someone would see the car with blood all over it and Nick and Deedee in the back barely breathing. I picked up the cell phone and called Danny. "I need help," I almost whispered. "Is everything okay?" I said "no" then silence fell on both ends. Finally he asked me where I was, I told him the street we were on. I was gonna tell him what happened when he told me to meet him at a nearby motel right off Bird Road.

Not able to hold it any longer, I just started to cry. I tried to talk but Danny wouldn't let me say anything. Out of the blue, he started talking about putting together a party for his nephew and asking me suggestions. At first I was thinking, this man must be crazy, but then I remembered the different conversation we practiced as cover up in case something came up. This way our conversation could never incriminate us, and it took our mind off of whatever went wrong and calmed us down. I went along with the game all the while praying that Nick and Deedee would be okay.

The motel seemed abandoned when I pulled into the parking lot. Three compact cars were parked next to each other close to the only lighted room with a neon green office sign. I drove to the back as instructed and a police car was sitting there. My heart dropped and thought for sure I was done then I realized it was Tim. He rushed to the car opened the passenger door and asked, "Where's Jerry?" My head resting on the steering wheel and through my sobs I whimpered, "He's dead."

Tim opened the passenger door and Nick whispered "get Deedee I…" then started coughing. "Alright bro," Tim said. As he headed toward the back stairs with Deedee over his shoulder and one of the briefcases in hand he looked toward me and said "Angel help Nick out the car." I made my way around the car and was welcomed by a graffiti of dry blood all over the car. I opened the back door and helped Nick out of the car as he stood holding on to the open door he said, "Grab the case." I followed his eyes to the front passenger seat to the black briefcase dropped earlier by Jerry. My eyes were now filled with tears. Nick kept his left hand pressed on his chest then with his right arm wrapped around my neck, and we followed Tim upstairs.

The room had two full size beds adjacent to each other separated by a night-stand. Deedee was already on the bed furthest from the door. As I helped Nick down on the empty bed, Tim said, "Danny's coming with a doctor, let's start cleaning them up." I'm not sure where else Nick had been hit, but his clothes were soaked with blood. I looked as injured as he was from all the blood I now had on my clothes from helping him up the stairs.

Without a word, Tim came over to Nick and I went up to Deedee. Her eyes were closed and her left arm covered with blood was hanging off the bed. I grabbed her hand and found her fingers somewhat cold. I ran to the closet and grabbed a spare fleece blanket to cover her up. Nick's jacket which still covered her body was saturated with blood and, as I pulled off the jacket one bullet hole after another revealed itself with a clear view of Deedee's internal organs. My hands rushed all over her body looking for a pulse or any signs of life but all I got was warm blood and semi-cold flesh. My head started to spin and for a second I thought I was gonna throw up. I looked at Deedee's face and I instantly became numb. I threw myself over her body and cried, "She's dead, she's dead."

Silence filled the room. Tim who was in the process of helping Nick out of his dirty clothes, looked up with his mouth dropped in shock. Nick was instantly next to the bed trying to get me off Deedee. I rolled off the bed onto the floor covered with blood. Nick dropped over Deedee, pressed his ears to her chest, felt her neck then pulled Deedee's lifeless body into his arms and cried like I never thought he could. Tim walked over to the TV and turned it on to cover up the piercing cries coming from Nick and me.

It wasn't long before Danny walked in with a guy who I presumed was the doctor. The guy wore a light blue long sleeve Guevara shirt and looked like one of those Hialeah doctors you'd normally see getting busted on the news for working out of his garage without a license. "What's going on?" asked Danny. "Deedee's dead," Tim replied rubbing his head. "Oh fuck," said Danny walking over to Nick. "Nick needs to be cleaned up, he's got a couple holes in his chest," said Tim.

The doctor placed his bag on the nightstand and ordered Nick to the other bed where he could take a look at him. Nick didn't look like he had any intention of moving away from Deedee. Danny literally had to pry her out of his arms as Tim pulled him away to the other bed. As Nick was being dragged, something came over me and I leaped around Tim sucker punched Nick right onto the bed and screamed, "You fucking bastard, it's all you fault." Danny rushed over and grabbed me as I tried to kick Nick who was now being held down by Tim and the doctor. "She kept telling you that Louis was following her why din'…" I cried. "I quita de Ahi!" (*Get her out of here*) yelled the doctor.

Danny held on to me and took me in the bathroom as I continued to kick and cry. He pressed my head into his chest still holding me with his other hand and kept saying, "You gotta calm down mama, you need to calm down." Even if I wanted to I don't think I could calm down, my body was shaking uncontrollably. "I can't believe this happened," I sobbed, "I saw Louis going up, and then people started shooting…Jer…ry's dead, Deedee's dead and…" He cut in before I could finish and said "Samantha, I gotta go take care of things. Do you think you can…?" Now it was my turn to cut in and told him I'd be okay. He went out the door and I stayed alone in the bathroom trying to compose myself.

Minutes later I followed Danny into the room. The curtains and windows were closed, the air was blasting and the man in the blue shirt was sewing Nick up while Danny talked to Nick in Spanish. Deedee was now covered with the fleece blanket with her hair exposed; I kneeled down next to her and quietly cried and whimpered as I stroked her hair. As much as I was hurting, the reality of Deedee being dead didn't seem to really sink in.

The front door opened and it was Tim. He looked at Danny and said, "It's gone." I'm not sure how I knew he was talking about the car but I quickly said, "my bag's in there." "Nah," said Tim. "I brought it up," pointing to my small black bag on the floor in the corner.

Tim looked at Danny and asked, "All right bro, you ready?" Danny started to get up and Nick, with red shuteyes and great effort, tried to grab Tim to stop him from moving her. Danny got up and said, "don't worry man it'll be alright." I watched Danny come toward the bed where Deedee laid. He picked up her body careful not to drop the cover. Tim helped complete a full body wrap up with the end of the blanket and they headed out the door.

I was trying to figure out what was going on, because it felt like a bunch of things were going on and most of it was going over my head. I followed them to the door and asked "What are you guys gonna do with her?" Danny was already outside; Tim who was right behind him gently pushed me back and said, "We'll be right back, just stay put." He pulled the door closed and moments later I heard a car leaving the parking lot.

I lowered myself to the now empty bed and numbly flipped through the TV channels and zoned out completely. Some time went by, the TV was starting to give me a headache so I got up to turn the volume down and as I reached for the knob a phone went off. The unexpected noise startled me and I panicked even more when I realized it was coming from my bag on the floor. Thinking it must be Danny calling for further instructions I quickly fetched the phone out of my bag and answered. It was Anthony. "Fuck" I thought "not today." As he continued to say hello I debated whether to answer or not. Then I heard myself say. "Anthony what a surprise." "Did I catch you at a bad time?" he asked. "Nah, nah" I lied "uh, uh what's up?" I said trying to compose myself. "I, I needed to talk to you." I tried calling you at home and even tried your, your job but…" "You called the club?" I cut in. "I don't work there anymore," I said. "That's what they told me…you don't sound to good, are you sure you're okay?" he asked. I looked over at the empty bed where Deedee earlier laid my voice started to crack and through silent tears I hoarsely replied, "I'm okay." Just then Nick started coughing.

"Damn it," I grumbled softly through my teeth. I'm not sure why I panicked but Anthony instantly sensed it and said, "I'm sorry I didn't realize you had company." I thought of something to say because clearly I couldn't tell him where I was or what was going on but then Nick tried to move and the pain from his wound must have kicked in and he let out one of those sounds that could easily be wrongly interpreted without knowing what was going on. "Maybe some other time when you can talk…" he said with controlled anger in his voice. "Anthony wait" I pleaded but he'd already hang up the phone.

All this time I waited to hear from him and he had to pick now to call. "If we had a chance I'm sure it's all over now," I thought to myself. I looked over at Nick with stitches, gauze cloth and bandages on his chest, tears seemed to be gliding down his face you could tell he was hurting but at this point I didn't care. I couldn't even sympathize with him all I felt toward him was hatred.

I leaned against the wall and slid to the floor my hands covered with dry blood covered my face as I sobbed violently. So much went through my head. I wished this whole thing was a nightmare, then at least I'd be able to wake up but it wasn't, this was real. Deedee was dead, Jerry was dead, Anthony was gone and I was wishing I was dead. I didn't know how much more of this I could take.

I was still on the floor when Danny came back holding a duffel bag. "We gotta get out of here," he said, "I got some changing clothes for you guys so let's make it fast." He threw me a black long sleeve T-shirt and some blue jeans and as he pulled out the clothes intended for Nick I went into the bathroom to change and clean up. When I came out the bathroom Nick was gone along with Raoul the doctor. Danny was sitting on one of the beds waiting. "What did you guys do with Deedee?" I asked. He gave me one of his authoritative looks and said, "Let it go."

"What the hell is that supposed to mean?" I asked. He didn't answer and grabbed a spray container off the floor next to the bed and asked if I'd used the towels in there. I was getting so fed up with these unanswered questions and whatever else was going on that I could kill somebody, the worse part was I was going through this sober. Danny was looking at me as if waiting for an answer so I said, "I took a shower what the hell do you think?" He got up and went into the bathroom but before he closed the door behind him he said, "Stay put don't touch anything." When he came out he packed the towels in the duffel bag with our bloody clothes, looked around and calmly said, "Let's go."

CHAPTER 14

Over the dark blue van the sky was big and still and full of moonlight. Raoul, who sewed Nick up, was in the front seat driving, Nick was in the second row holding on to the seat. Not wanting to be near Nick, I was in the back with Danny and the two briefcases with Tim in his patrol car behind the van. We drove for what seemed like an eternity. Tears were periodically rolling down my face and Danny who now had his arm around me kept rubbing my shoulder without a word. We drove quietly into the night on the Florida Turnpike and finally a sign reading "Florida City" came up and Danny said, "Were almost there."

It wasn't long before we got off the highway, about a mile off the main road. We swayed to the left into a deeper darkness, the bounciness and broken gravel that ricocheted off the underside of the van indicated that we were no longer on a paved road and finally pulled into a driveway canopied with overgrown palm trees. My body all of a sudden tensed up and wondered, "what if they kill me?" I started to pull away from Danny but he held on tight and whispered in my ear "It's okay, it's okay."

Raoul got out and came around the van as he slid the door open a chorus of deep growl and four pairs of bright eyes came charging toward him. He yelled something in Spanish and the dogs whimpered away. Danny jumped off carrying the two briefcases. I hurried into the darkness trying to keep up with their giant steps as the gravel fidgeted under my feet all the while hoping that the dogs wouldn't attack me.

We walked through an oversized door that led into a large dimly lit room overly decorated with gold-framed mirrors in tasteless red. There were two large couches covered with a tropical flower like pattern embedded in a deep red; a rich red velvet armchair across the door with two cherry-wood end tables on either side. In places where I assumed there would be a window were lavish curtains in red and gold. An armoire in the corner displayed an open armed statue of the Virgin Mary with Santa Maria lighted candles around it. Upon our entrance, a short and chubby, yet curvy woman who seemed to have been expecting us calmly welcomed us in Spanish and gestured for us to sit. Raoul said something to her in Spanish and disappeared into a back room with Tim and a barely conscious Nick. Danny moved closer to the woman and said, "Buenos noches, Teresa." "Buenos noches, Danny, something to drink? Non?" she asked then looked toward me. "Teresa," Danny said, "this is…" he paused as if wondering which name to use then quickly said "Angel." I extended my hand toward her. She grabbed my hand and instead of shaking it, she pulled me in and kissed me on both sides of my cheek and said, "Ah Angel, nice to meet choo." I said, "Nice to meet you too, Theresa." "Tey rey sa!" She corrected me with a smile. "Teresa," I repeated. She disappeared into the hallway leading to the back of the house yelling in her heavy Spanish accent "I bring some cof-fee." "That's Raoul's wife," Danny said to me.

We were now joined with Tim and Raoul and Teresa now holding a stainless steel coffee kettle with toy-like teacups. Without asking who wanted coffee she started pouring. Danny was the first to reach for the coffee. "Gracias Teresa," he said. Tim and Raoul were handed theirs, then she came closer to me for mine. "Thank you," I said shyly wishing for something stronger than coffee.

The sound of the night filled the room. Danny asked Raoul about Nick's condition which according to him, a full recovery was expected. Danny wanted to know how soon they'd be able to travel but Raoul suggested at least a full week. He then walked over to a corner cabinet and pulled out two bottles of Jack Daniels. Teresa disappeared on queue and fetched five glasses out of their kitchen. I sat quietly fuming at the thought that Deedee was dead and these people didn't seem to be taking it seriously; it's as if it wasn't sinking in. My thoughts were still on Deedee who was my drinking partner, and I could feel the tears filling up my eyes. I grabbed the glass that was given to me. I extended my arm in the air and thought to myself, "Here's to you Deedee." With a strong bite, the whiskey went down leaving a warm sensation all over my body. I quickly emptied my glass that was soon refilled by Teresa. After a few glasses Raoul told us that our rooms were ready and that he was calling it a night. It had been a long day, every inch of my body was hurting and I missed my bed. As Raoul disappeared into the hallway with Teresa, I looked around and thought how pathetic and out of control my life had become. Here I was stuck in a room with a corrupted police officer, two major drug dealers, and now my best friend is dead. I didn't even want the money anymore; I just wanted my life back.

"Danny," I said, "I'm tired. When can I go home?" He looked over at Tim and said "not tonight Angel." Tim got up and said, "All right guys, I got a long shift tomorrow, I gotta get some sleep. I'll give you a buzz before work." He gave Danny one of those brotherly handshake/hugs, kissed me on the cheek, and headed for the door. I was so angry I couldn't even see straight. "How come he gets to go home?" I asked with all the might left in me. Tim sensing drama coming near took his chance and exited the room.

"What the fuck is this? You can't just hold me here." "Stop yelling, he said in between his teeth "Ain't nobody kidnapping you. Look I didn't plan for this shit to happen. I'm just dealing the deck that was handed to me so lay the fuck off!" For an instant we were silent then he went on, "I gotta stay here with Nick and I can't leave you alone until I know we're in the clear!" He threw up his hands in exasperation and said, "What the hell, Samantha, give it till tomorrow." He sounded and looked exhausted so I decided to let it go. "Where am I sleeping?" I asked more calmly. He was already heading toward the hallway and without looking at me he said "Just follow me I'll show you to your room." "Wait," I said bending over the open bottle on the end table. I filled up my glass and when I turned around Danny was standing right behind me. He filled up his glass as I did, raised his glass at me and said "good idea."

The décor in the room was complementary in taste with the living room. Everything was black and green. Danny sensed my hesitation to go in. "I'll be across the hall" he said pointing to a closed door about eight feet from mine. My room was filled with folkloric masks I got in the bed leaning my back against the head board as my body tried to convince my mind that it was okay to lie down and sleep. I was just about to doze off when an owl clock from the far left corner of the room scared the shit out of me by announcing the fourth hour of the morning with a sharp piercing sound. Leaving my shoes behind I grabbed my purse and ran out the door into Danny's room.

He was sitting shirtless on a chair, his eyes fixed on the briefcases filled with money opened on the floor. He slowly looked up and without me having to say anything he said, "You're not getting the bed." "Then take me home," I said as I walked over to the bed and got under the covers. The bed and the pillows felt cold but I was so tired that I was beyond caring. When I woke up, the sun was filtering through the window and an unshaven Danny was sitting on the opposite side of the bed. "It made the news," he said.

That short comment mentally brought me back to yesterday, and everything that happened rushed back into my mind. I turned to look at the TV screen and the news was on. The morning anchor was talking about an alligator found in a residential canal nothing about the shooting. "What did they say?" I asked. "They haven't covered the details; that should be coming up. They just showed the scene in the news highlights. I'm gonna watch it with Nick," he said heading for the door.

I was so tired of them acting like I wasn't part of this mess when they wouldn't even let me go home. I hopped off the bed and said, "I'm coming with you." He didn't say anything but as I headed out the door, I realized that my shoes were left in the room across the hall. I rushed over, grabbed my shoes and followed him to Nick's room which was further down the hallway.

Nick was a pathetic sight. He was sitting in bed looking like he'd aged 20 years overnight. His eyes were still bloodshot as if he'd been crying all night; his unbuttoned shirt gave a clear view of the bandages that he was wrapped up with. The look on his face reminded me of the fact that Deedee was gone and automatically my eyes were filled with tears, not for Nick, because at this time I still couldn't bring myself to forgive him because I'd lost the only friend I had. He looked up when we walked in and neither one of us said a word. Danny went around the other side of the bed and sat on a wicker chair next to the bed. I went to the end of the bed and halfway propped myself up looking straight into the TV screen. It was less than two minutes when the reporter came up with the news.

"We're back reporting live from a shooting that authorities are calling "a divorce gone bad." Dianna Palverra was visiting with some friends last night where she was shot by her husband Juan Louis Diaz; the two were in the process of getting a divorce. Not wanting to go through with the divorce Juan Louis Diaz showed up last night with the signed divorce papers, shot his wife along with her friends and finally turned the gun on himself. This is a real tragedy. Neighbors reported the gunshots late last night and now you can see the authorities moving the bodies from the scene of the incident." A woman who apparently lived nearby was interviewed quoting, "I can't believe this kind of thing would happen here. This is such a nice quiet neighborhood, you just never know these days."

My eyes were now filled with tears as a picture of the victims, including Deedee, propped on the screen. The reporter went on to say that they were waiting for family members to come forward and claim the bodies.

Nick, Danny and I were all quiet as we watched the pictures on the screen and the reporters moved on to the next fatal news of the day. We sat there in awe. My mind was racing trying to figure out how these boys had managed to get Deedee's body back to the scene so this story would pan out. Nothing was mentioned about drug deals or anything. The two buyers who were shot were reported as friends that Deedee was visiting.

I turned around to ask "how...?" "Don't worry about it" Danny interrupted, "it should be safe for us to go home now." "We're safe," I repeated whispering "isn't that swell and Deedee is dead but I guess that's the trade off for all that money." Danny got off the chair furiously and started to yell. "You know what Samantha, fuck you! Ain't nobody forced you into this so get off your high horse of virtue." Nick surprisingly tried to cut in to calm things down but Danny wasn't hearing it. "Nah, I'm tired of this shit. I didn't kill Deedee, nobody was planning for Deedee or Jerry to be dead so stop the freaking guilt trip, it was a fucking accident. Nobody told her to marry Louis. If he didn't show up last night everything would have been fine." "You don't say!" I replied back. "If you guys, especially Nick, had believed her when she kept saying that Louis was following her and done something about it, this would have been prevented!" Danny got right up in my face and said "Well since you cared so fucking much why didn't YOU do something about it?"

His words struck a nerve and it was all I could do from launching at him. I stormed out into the hallway to the room where I was supposed to sleep. I sat on the bed with silent tears washing down my face and thought how right Danny was, why didn't I do something about it? I've been so absorbed with Anthony and whatever else was going in my life that I didn't even think of trying to help Deedee, the closest thing I had to a family. I don't know what I could have done but now it was too late to find out.

I had to get out of here. I brushed my hand over my hair, grabbed my purse and headed for the front room. Teresa was sitting on one of the couches drinking coffee with a magazine. She closed the book as I drew near and said "Buenos Dias, Angel, some coffee for you?" I composed myself said hello to her and politely declined the coffee invitation. "I need a taxi, I need to get home," I said slowly fighting back my tears. "Taxi?" she replied getting up from the couch. She stopped, thought for a moment as if trying to think of the right word to say then finally said. "No, no," then disappeared down the hallway. I didn't have time for this; I just wanted to go home.

Without thinking, I stormed out the heavy doors but before I could reach halfway down the driveway, I was ambushed by four angry dogs. I stood frozen empowered by fear as vicious teeth growled at me. The voice of Raoul kind of reassured me that maybe I would be okay but for a second it didn't seem like the dogs wanted to move. I kept my eyes halfway closed blinded with tears and finally after a few words in Spanish coming from Raoul, the dogs calmed down and reluctantly went away. In his accented English he asked me if I was okay and signaled me to follow him. Feeling defeated, I followed his steps back into the house. I was starting to think it was impossible to leave this place. I felt like I was living the lyrics to *Hotel California* by the Eagles. Danny was in the living room with Teresa when we came back in. He looked at me and said in between coffee sips "Tim's on his way to get us."

The look on Danny's face was so cold and distant that it chilled me to the bone. For the first time since I've known these boys, I saw them for what they really were and it scared me. If they could use Deedee like that, to cover up their asses, I'm sure they wouldn't even think twice about doing something to me. Besides, my relationship to them was through Deedee so if there was any loyalty toward me, which I doubt, I'm sure it's out the window.

I placed myself on the couch and at this point I didn't even know how to feel or react. I just didn't wanna be here. I sat quietly on that couch for at least a good hour before Tim finally showed up. We all got in his car, Danny in the front, Nick and I in the back, then drove to the warehouse where my car was left from the night before.

I'd never been so happy to see my apartment; I never thought I'd be alive to see this place again. When I checked my phone, most of the girls from the club and some of my customers who knew Deedee left several messages trying to find out what happened. I was in no mood to talk to anyone so I made a mental note to call them later and jumped in the shower for a much needed freshening up.

CHAPTER 15

Nick was in pretty bad shape so a few days went by before he was functioning enough to make any decision about Deedee's funeral arrangements and her family in Argentina. Deedee's mother and uncle were doing the necessary paperwork to get a visa for their trip to the United States. Their intention was to take Deedee's body back to Argentina so she could be buried in their family grave. As we waited for Deedee's family to get here, Nick arranged for a wake and a local memorial service since we obviously couldn't go to Argentina for the funeral.

The day before the wake, Nick called and asked if I could help out with the wake since I was Deedee's closest friend. We were still on not so good terms but we had the mutual understanding that our differences could be put aside and do whatever needed to be done for Deedee. The following day, Deedee's wake filled up her penthouse with about twenty to thirty people coming from the viewing at the funeral home. Nick sat on the balcony the entire time just looking down into the parking lot. He was chain smoking through a pack of cigarettes and sipping a flask of whiskey. The only time he'd say a word was when he was spoken to. Nick's two sisters were helping me host the wake making sure that everybody was taken care of. For some strange reason, Danny brought one of his girlfriends along and from the moment she got there it was a constant nagging of "how long are we gotta stay here?" or "are we leaving any time soon?" In my mind I was wondering why he would bring one of his girlfriends to the wake when the girl barely knew Deedee and didn't even want to be here in the first place. To top it off she didn't even have the decency to show some respect.

A lot of the girls from the club were there and Danny being a regular at the Unicorn knew most of them. They had entertained him at one point or another. Throughout the night, every time one of the girls came over to talk to Danny, his girlfriend would cop an attitude, cut into the conversation, or just pull Danny away.

By 10:30 P.M. the guests were gone leaving the cleaning crew: Nick's two sisters and I. Danny was on the balcony with Nick and Danny's girlfriend was in the living room on her cell phone. As soon as we were done with the clean up and Nick's sisters had left, I started feeling the pain that I'd been trying to avoid. I went into Deedee's room to gather my stuff and the outside lights were filtering in through the window leaving bird-like shadows on the wall. I looked around the room, let out a heavy breath as memories of happy times shared in this place with Deedee rushed through my mind. I opened the dresser's top drawer to retrieve my keys and grabbed Deedee's keys instead. I looked at the set of keys held together by a small silver square frame in a leather pouch. I pushed the frame out of its case and found a picture of Nick and Deedee taken last Christmas and a picture of me and her taken at one of those instant cameras at the mall. The emptiness of the room suddenly closed around me. I lowered myself to the ground against the bed as my eyes burned with tears. On the floor in the dimly lit room I realized how grateful I was for the few hours of the wake when I was able to take my mind off of things. I held on to the keychain staring at the picture, trying to relive the memories of that day. My pain was overpowering but I had no more energy to fight it off and now my uncontrollable sobbing was evidence of that. I'm not sure how long I was on the floor when I heard someone coming out of the bathroom, which was next door to the room. I looked up and was caught off guard by Danny in the doorway. We hadn't been on speaking terms since the incident at Raoul's place and I was in no mood to deal with him. I needed some tissue to clean up my face but I didn't think my legs could be trusted to hold me up so I opted for the front of my shirt. In two leaps Danny was on the floor next to me. Without a word he drew his arm around my shoulder and pulled me close to him. "I'm sorry Samantha, about what I said to you and how everything with Deedee was handled," he said. My pain didn't leave me room to think of the hatred or whatever disagreement existed between us, I held on to him and continued to cry. "What the fuck is going on here?" Said Danny's "girlfriend" Veronica. She was standing in the middle of the room looking like she was witnessing a crime. Without either one of us acknowledging her presence in the room, I eased out of Danny's arm trying to compose myself. Danny was getting off the floor still looking toward me when I saw her grab the small jewelry box off the dresser to throw at me. Sitting Indian style on the floor was not the best position to be in when you were being attack. I screamed and tilted out of the way and as the box hit the wall, Danny thankfully grabbed her before she could grab something else. I was now on my feet, my sobbing and decomposure took a back seat as heated blood rushed to my head. I sure could use an outlet for my anger and pains so if this bitch was in the mood for drama, she could bring it on. As she tried to swing at me, Danny pushed Veronica out the room and stood behind the door so I couldn't come out as the two of them went at it. "What the hell are you doing pulling some shit like that?" yelled Danny. "What the hell are you doing making out with that bitch?" she yelled in reply. "You freaking psycho, ain't nobody was making out, this is a freaking wake you…" She cut in still yelling "I don't give a fuck what it is, you've been ignoring me all night acting like Mister Player and now this, you know what? Take me home, I'm done with your ass, take me home." "Take you home?" Danny repeated in disbelief "ain't nobody stopping you, go home, I told you I had shit to…" I pushed against the door hoping it'd give way but Danny was still holding it shut. Before he could finish his sentence I heard a slap or someone getting hit then Veronica yelling "you just wanna be with that bitch." "Veronica," I heard Danny say two octaves lower than his normal voice "get your shit and leave before I hit you back."

I'm not sure what was going on but I heard Veronica's voice fading toward the door as she screamed for Danny to let go of her and then the door slammed. Things were suddenly quiet but my heart was still beating fast ready for a good fight. I needed a beer to calm myself down before I could leave. After awhile, I left the room and headed for the kitchen where I found Danny pouring Johnnie Walker Black Label. He took one look at me, handed me the highball glass and then fetched another glass for himself. He raised his glass slightly at me and said, "I'm sorry about that. I don't even know why I brought her along." This time it was Nick who calmly interrupted and said, "Bro, I think Veronica is fucking up your car down there. Danny listened to the sound and confirmed that it was his alarm. He raced out of the apartment followed by Nick and minutes later they were in the parking lot. I went to the bedroom window where I could have an unobstructed view of the scene. Veronica was down there keying Danny's Mercedes and busting the side windows. Being far off the ground and with the alarm sound, it was hard to hear the words being yelled back and forth but suddenly Veronica punched Danny across the face and this time Danny did not hesitate to hit her back. "Holy shit," I thought, "I can't believe he hit her back."

Nick tried to pull Danny away but Veronica kept on swinging at him. People were coming out to their balconies to see what was going on. As the fight and the argument died out, I dropped down on the bed to face the dresser where Deedee's picture stood "Just like you to have drama at your wake," I said out loud at the picture. Someone must have called the building security because the yellow lights were flashing through the window. Finally, security called Veronica a cab to go home, the car alarm was turned off and neighbors were back inside.

I was ready to leave when Nick and Danny came in. Danny's shirt was ripped along the shoulder and his face red flushed with anger. I looked at them both and said "I better go; I'll see you guys in the morning."

As I headed for the door Nick broke his silence again and said, "I got a couple of limos for..." he paused awkwardly searching for the right words "the families...we could pick you up if you want." We looked at each other, feeling the pain we shared. I almost started to cry but before tears could fill my eyes I nodded my head at him and said, "That would be nice," then turned away and rushed out the door.

CHAPTER 16

The church pews were filled with Deedee's neighbors, Nick's friends and family, Deedee's mother and uncle who got in earlier that morning, girls from the club and even some customers. The overabundance of flower arrangements spilled their fragrance into the air. The whole service seemed so out of character for Deedee's farewell but Nick was barely functioning so the people he decided to put in charge didn't know Deedee enough to do otherwise. The priest was brief and impersonal and toward the end, Deedee's mother read a eulogy in Spanish? As I looked around, I felt like I was the only one feeling the impact of the loss of a loved one, a feeling that had become my norm. Our next stop was the cemetery where a memorial stone was erected in Deedee's memory.

I rode in the limo to the cemetery with Nick, one of Nick's sisters, Deedee's mother and her uncle. Most of the people from the church were already there when we reached our destination. The crowd merged on either side of the casket that was filled with a picture of Deedee, along with some of her favorite things. A last prayer was read and the casket was lowered into the ground. A couple of people got closer and dropped stems of roses as their last farewell. Deedee's mom was being held by her brother as her emotions took over her body. My face was covered with tears, I felt a sense of déjà vu. Scenes from my father's funeral rushed through my mind and for a moment I didn't know which emotion was sharper, all I know was that my heart couldn't take any more pain.

Sleep never came for me the night of the funeral. My pain and sorrows were dealt with by drinking beer and tequila in hopes that I'd pass out and never wake up. By the crack of dawn it was obvious that I didn't have enough alcohol to numb my pain so in defeat I cried myself hoarse wishing I had Anthony to help me through this.

The ringing of the phone forced me up. I laid there taking in the fact that I'd fallen asleep. The persistence of the rings forced me out of bed to the receiver on the kitchen counter. "Where are you?" said Danny on the other end sounding somewhat inpatient. "Hey," I hoarsely replied feeling the effect of my drinking "what are…" "Samantha," Danny cut in without changing his tone, "you were supposed to be here an hour ago." I suddenly remembered yesterday when Nick asked me to come by. "I'm sorry," I said rubbing the sleep out of my eyes "I'm…I'll leave right now."

When I got there I noticed Nick, Danny and Tim's cars in the driveway and for a second I wondered whether or not I should go in. I'm not sure what it was but since Deedee died and me knowing so much, I've been freaking out thinking that they might do something to me to make sure I didn't blow the whistle on them. What the hell, I finally thought, if they really want to do something to me I'm sure they'd know where to find me. I sat in my car playing the what if game but in the end it didn't seem like I had a choice. The front door was unlocked so after knocking a few times I opened the door and followed the voices into the room. Looking around the place, all of Nick's furniture was gone except for a few chairs on the patio where the three of them sat. "Hey guys," I said softly. They raised their bottles in response as I grabbed one of the empty chairs. For some strange reason, Deedee's absence came at me hard as I noticed the fact that I was the only female there. "Is anybody else coming?" I asked, as I pushed back my tears. Nick let out a deep sigh as he rubbed his side where the bandages were exposed through his thin shirt and said, "Nah…Deedee's mom and uncle are at the hotel." "Oh," I said quietly. "Anyway," Nick went on "I'm leaving with them tomorrow with the body."

I looked at the other two, wondering why he's telling me about his plans then back at Danny making sure I heard him right. Tim and Danny were smoking and sipping their beer quietly. I started to say what happened to Belize but then I realized that the place they were supposed to get married might not be a place he'd want to go. I looked toward Tim and Danny and reluctantly asked, "what about you guys?" Danny was the one who answered as Nick got up to get me a beer. "Tim's staying; I'll be leaving some time next week." He didn't say where he was going and I wasn't sure whether to ask or not. "We need to split the money" Danny went on "unless there's an objection," he said looking at me. "We should split Deedee's cut five ways and give Jerry's wife his cut." We all looked at each other, obviously in agreement. "When is Jerry's funeral?" I asked feeling guilty for not asking sooner. "The day after tomor-row," answered Tim, "his wife doesn't want us there," he quickly added. Jerry's wife never approved of his hanging out with the boys so her decision wasn't much of a surprise.

Moments later we were in Nick's bedroom, the only furnished room in the house. I'd never seen so much money in my life. The split must have been done before I got there because lying on the bed were five bags filled with 50's and 100 dollars bills. Nick pulled one of his legs up the bed with his back resting against the headboard. "The green bag is yours, Samantha," he said pointing toward the open bag. "There's 1.5 million dollars in there," Danny said, "you're more than welcome to count it if you want."

I did a quick look at Danny, for some reason I resented his comment but mostly his tone of voice. Feeling my discomfort, both Tim and Nick looked toward Danny with reproaching stares. "I'm sorry," he said, "I didn't mean..." I didn't even let him finish. I turned toward Nick and heard myself say, "I don't think I can take it." I could feel the three pairs of eyes staring at me as Nick asked in disbelief, "What do you mean you can't take it? Don't pay attention to Danny, that's your share of the deal." My eyes never left Nick. I couldn't believe what I was saying but as the words came out I knew them to be true. "This has nothing to do with Danny," I said trying to hold back my tears "Deedee was your girl but she was the closest thing I had as a family," I looked toward the open bag filled with money and in my mind I could see Deedee's blood all over it. Suddenly, conscious of my tears, I lowered my eyes to the floor and softly said, "I can't." The room was quiet for a while as the boys looked at each other. At last Nick took a deep breath and tried to change the subject by asking me what I was gonna do. The question that's been running through my head was said out loud. "I'm not sure," I answered, "probably find a job, and go back to school." Danny started to say something then changed his mind. I looked around the room, remembering the many parties that took place there and finally said "I guess that's it guys." More out of fear than anything else, I moved toward Tim and Danny gave each of them a goodbye and good luck hug and as they left the room I went up to Nick, holding on to his chest, his eyes filled up with tears but this time he didn't try to hide them. "Throw her a rose for me in Argentina, okay?" "You got it," he said in the best voice he could find.

My face was now a mess so before I left, I excused myself to the bathroom. My heart was beating fast as I patted my face dry with the tissue. I can't believe I just turned down 1.5 million dollars. But deep down I knew I didn't have a choice, I needed a clean slate and hanging on to the old one would make it impossible to move on. Besides I had some money in the bank I could always find a job, I would just have to find a way to make it last. I got out of the bathroom with renewed strength, I went back to the room to say goodbye. Nick was sitting in the room with a new lit cigarette I said goodbye and wished him luck again.

On my way out the door, I found Danny and Tim in the kitchen doing a couple of lines on the kitchen counter. "These boys never quit," I thought. I waited for them to sniff it all in and said my last goodbyes.

As I got in my car, my heart was beating faster than my engine. I wondered whether I'd just bought myself out of this clan or dug myself deeper into a hole. Without even thinking, I got on the Palmetto Expressway heading toward Deedee's memorial place. Suddenly I felt an urgency to get out of South Florida. I'd been beating my head trying to decide what to do or where I could go to get away, this time I shocked myself with the answer. "I'm going back home," I heard myself say. "This town has cost me enough;" I thought. A smile came on my face at the irony of it all. I spent most of my life working hard at getting out of Georgia and now I was ready to run back. "Yeah," I said out loud as if to convince myself, "I need a fresh start and Georgia is the only other place I know."

A slow rhythmic drizzle was coming down as I pulled my car into the lot. I bought two bouquets of wild flowers at the entrance and headed down the grass pathway for the headstone. It had been less than 48 hours and already the Florida weather had some loose grass and dirt lying across the memorial tombstone. Tears were slowly running down my face, I lowered myself to the ground, brushed off the headstone before laying down the flowers. "I'm going home girl," I said softly, "can you believe it? Going back to Georgia!" I paused for a while as if waiting for an answer knowing darn well that I wouldn't get one. "I miss you…I really miss you, I'm scared and alone," I sobbed out, "I don't know what I'm gonna do without you. I didn't take the money. I know you probably think I'm crazy…I don't know girl, I just couldn't, your blood is all over that money…oh Deedee, if only we could go back."

My heart was in so much pain not just for Deedee but for all that I've lost in the last few months. I went home to a half bottle of Rum to get me through the night with no intention of sleeping. By early dawn, I had packed two suitcases with the few things that I wanted to take with me from my apartment. My furniture, dance costumes and attire and some of the clothes that I knew were not Georgia appropriate was all left behind. It was a deliberate act to leave as much of Florida behind as possible. Finally, I sat down with my coffee cup before going to the building manager to turn in my keys. Tom, the building manager, was playing solitaire on the computer when I walked through the office door. He stretched out lazily as he pivoted his chair around toward me. "What's up Samantha?" I forced a smile on my face as I pulled the keys out of my pocket and said, "I'm going away so I'm here to return my keys." "Return your keys? For going away? You mean you're moving?" "I guess you could say that," I replied. Tom was now up leaning against the front desk where I stood and said, "I'm sorry about your friend, she was something wasn't she?" "Yes she was," I said thoughtfully as I remembered the times when Deedee would bring Tom a couple of six packs with a couple of joints or would join him on the roof for a quick smoke. We were both quiet for a moment and finally he said, "Let me get the paper work." Tom went to the file cabinet and as he looked for my file he went on talking. "You know you'll lose your deposit for breaking the lease?" That was common knowledge but I went ahead and answered him anyway. "I know, besides most of my stuff is still up there so you can use the deposit to get that stuff out of there." Reading through the folder that he'd just pulled out he said, "I don't think we'll need $5,400 to clean up the place so if you leave a forward address, we can mail you the difference.

The words $5,400 jiggled my mind since I only recall writing a check for $1,800 dollars to Stanley which was to cover the first and last month plus security. "Are you sure you're looking at my files?" I asked. He pulled the cover down and quietly read the name "Samantha L. Goldsmith?" "Yeah, but I didn't put $5,400 down," I said. He placed the folder on the desk and turned it around for me to see the forms as he went over them. "The lease agreement was $1,200 a month and Mr. Wellington sent a check the last week of December for $7,200 which is the yearly difference from what you were paying. We are in May so the balance left is $4,200 plus the $1,200 dollars deposit that gives you $5,400. I stood there speechless at the thought that Stanley would go out of his way to do this and not even tell me about it. All this time I thought I was getting a good deal paying $600.00 a month for a luxury apartment in Coral Gables. I should have known this was too good to be true but for some reason I just assumed he knew the owner or something. Stanley might be generous but if there's one thing about him is that he hates irrational waste and throwing away $5,400 of his money is definitely something he wouldn't be happy about. "Do you know how much of the money will be used for compensation?" I asked, looking at Tom. "I don't know, it depends how much damage is in the apartment and how long it takes to get a new tenant," he answered. I pulled out my checkbook and said "if I write you a check can you see to it that Mr. Wellington gets it, and whatever is left you can mail it to me.

I got some paper from Tom and drafted a quick note to Stanley. Once my lease termination papers were signed, I told Tom I'd give him a call as soon as I get where I was going to give him the address where he could forward all my correspondence. He walked me to the door and wished me good luck as I walked out the door for the last time.

The sun seemed to be playing hide-and-go-seek as the miles off of 95 Expressway went by quickly each taking me further from Miami and closer to Georgia. My thoughts went back and forth between the future and the life I was leaving behind. When my emotions started to bring back my tears, I cranked up the music and pressed my foot down on the accelerator refusing to let my pains and uncertainty get the best of me. By the time I got to Vero Beach, my previous sleepless night and the lack of food were catching up with my body. Getting out of Florida seemed to be taking forever. The unchanging scenery made it seem like a never-ending road. Finally, I gave into exhaustion and pulled into one of the hotels off the expressway.

CHAPTER 17

Anthony walked out of Samantha's apartment feeling more hurt and betrayed than he thought possible. Why didn't she tell him she worked at the Unicorn? How could he have been so stupid and not see what was going. He didn't even see this one coming but as they say "the greater the love, the harder the heartache." And what bothered him most was how he had to find out about it. He felt like such a fool falling in love with Samantha and to find out that he never really knew her. And the worse part was he couldn't deny the fact that he still loved her. But how can he have a relationship with someone he couldn't trust.

Weeks went by and time, which was said to heal all things didn't seem to lessen the pain so Anthony buried himself in his work. Andrew and the boys who knew what happened tried everything they could to get his mind off things but nothing seemed to work. Subconsciously he kept hoping that she would call even as an attempt to amend the damage that was done but nothing. On a few occasions he thought about calling himself but the thought of the last time he called her bothered him so much that he avoided the idea. Andrew and Donald were throwing all kinds of girls at him telling him to just let go, if anyone should call anybody it should be Samantha after all she's the one who screwed up.

A few months went by and Anthony was slowly getting back into the dating game. For some reason, he couldn't seem to shake Samantha out of his system. No matter how many parties or clubs he let Andrew talk him into or how many extra hours he put into work, at the end of the day his thoughts would always drive back to Samantha. He wasn't sure whether the possibility of saving the relationship was there but just for his peace of mind, he wanted and needed to know who Samantha really was. Andrew couldn't understand what was going on in Anthony's mind but he knew if anyone could help him it would be their father. After all, they met Samantha through him.

The affect that the situation had on his son was evident when Stanley picked his son up from the Heathrow Airport. As a dad he was seeing Anthony as his teenage son going though a broken heart and his fatherly instinct was telling him to rush to his rescue. But Stanley knew better and as much as he wanted to help, he knew he had to let Anthony work though this on his own terms.

One morning, Anthony picked his dad up for their Wednesday Wellington golf ritual and Anthony finally decided to ask his father about Samantha. That day, on the green, Stanley told Anthony everything he knew about Samantha including some of the minor details that were shared with him in Samantha's last letter. He was one of the few people, other than Deedee who really had a chance to know Samantha while she was Angel. Stanley was careful not to come across as if taking sides or excusing Samantha's behavior; after all he hated seeing his son going through this. He told Anthony as much as he knew about her background, how she ended up where she was and a little bit about the deal that cost her, her best friend's life.

Before Anthony left he read Samantha's letter and instead of the peace and closure he was expecting from this trip, he was now confused with the mixed emotions about his father for knowing yet keeping all this from him when he knew how he felt about Samantha and even more confused about his feelings towards her. What he wanted was closure to this phase of his life yet despised everything his heart didn't seem to want to let go.

Upon his return to Florida, Anthony decided he would do whatever it took to get on with his life. The bottom line was he couldn't turn back the clock and no matter what, it still didn't change the fact that she lied to him. Besides, if Samantha did leave town according to her letter, what choice did he have?

Anthony met Abigail a little bit over a year after his break-up with Samantha and like all the other girls that he'd been dating ever since, she at first was no more than a casual relationship where they would go out, have dinners and share their beds with each other at their convenience. Out of the blue, Anthony's line of women disappeared and he was spending most of his time, sharing his bed with only Abigail. Andrew and the other guys could think of a few other girls they would rather see Anthony with. They just couldn't see what the two of them had in common but never the less they couldn't deny the fact that Abigail was gorgeous, financially secure, (thanks to her wealthy family) successful in her career as chief editor for a major magazine, and absolutely adored Anthony. The only thing Abigail seemed to love more than Anthony or life itself was herself, one of the things that most people didn't care for about her. She'd seize any chance she could to get in the spotlight. Only a man secure enough with himself would take the time to overlook Abigail's self-centeredness to see some of her more positive traits. Abigail was intelligent, strong-minded, very driven and focused and those were some of the things that Anthony liked about her. Those close to Anthony, especially Andrew, hated the fact that Abigail behaved as if she was in control of the relationship but Anthony would always reassure them that things were fine. "After all," he'd say, "it's not like we're getting married or anything." As far as everybody was concerned Anthony was happy and that's all that really mattered.

Seven months into the relationship, they were all in London celebrating Stanley's birthday when Abigail announced that she and Anthony got engaged. "When did you decide that?" Stanley asked Anthony later on that night when they were alone. "Couple of days ago," he said. "And this is what you want?" his father asked. "I believe so, I think Abigail's a great catch and we love each other so why not," replied Anthony. They were both quiet for a while; Anthony lost in thoughts looking through the window into the dark yard and Stanley looking at his son. "Are you in love with her?" asked Stanley. Anthony turned to look at the untouched Merlot he'd been holding in his hand and said, "I think I love her but can you ever be sure?" With that he got up and bid his father goodnight an as indication that the conversation was over.

CHAPTER 18

The dim lit streets of Georgia welcomed me with fresh washed roads from the recent rain and the aroma from the early flowers of spring. Not much seemed to have changed since I left or since the last time I was there which seemed like an eternity ago. As I drove through the familiar streets, I remembered the summers and spring picnics I used to hate but now brought sweet memories of dad laughing, the Christmas parades that dad and I religiously went to, the fall dance at the community centers, and Ms. Perry's house next to the cemetery which was famous for giving out the best candies to trick or treaters on Halloween. The church. The place where everything came together: learning, teaching, gossips and community. I breathed in the fresh air of the cool new arrived spring season. Everything seemed still as I drove down the dark street into the driveway. I waited for the motion light to turn on and soon realized that I had to make due with the moonlight. The bite of the fresh air that was nonexistent in Florida surrounded me the minute I stepped out the car. I grabbed my bags and decided to deal with the boxes in the morning. I opened the door and found the light switch next to it. I carried my stuff into the house, halfway expecting to see dad coming out of the kitchen to welcome me home and tell me how much he'd miss having me around. Knowing full well he had passed I could still feel his presence there. I looked around the room taking in the fact that it really was just going to be me, myself and I.

Everything was exactly as I had left it except for the spider webs occupying every corner of the rooms. The covered living room chairs, the grandfather clock which hadn't worked since I was in high school yet daddy wouldn't get rid of it because he was sure he could fix it, and the dining room table where the two of us often sat for dinner laid bare with a stack of old newspapers. I slowly exhaled, blinked back my tears and went through each room turning on every working light in the house. I dragged my bags to my old room, noticing all the work that the house needed. After unpacking, I stepped into the bathroom to get the water running for a much needed bath.

By the end of the week, everybody had been by the house checking for themselves that I was really back in town. They all had questions and wanted to know what my plans were. Was I on vacation or back for good? Not that I was ungrateful for people coming by but I grew up in this town so I knew what their motives were. I didn't have to search far to know that I was the new hot topic of the season but I was in no mood to satisfy their curiosity or give them anything to talk about.

I tried to be as civil as I could, yet saying as little as possible and declining any extended invitation while reminding myself I didn't owe anybody an explanation or an account for anything.

It wasn't long before I started to get the cold shoulder. It's as if they all expected me to come back and be the same innocent girl that I was before I left Georgia. Sometimes I'd hear the younger kids talking, undoubtedly from what they'd heard their parents referring to me as a "high nose big city girl." Or that I came back home because I couldn't make in the big city.

On one of her visits, Miss Greene, who both her and her husband had been close friends with Dad, gave me one of those Southern "you-better-listen-to-me kind of speech" "People round here are talking cha, saying that you came awed here talking all different, acting like you can't talk to nobody no more, keeping to yourself. Now I don't know how they do in the big city and all but you know we all family round here. Your daddy, God rest his soul, was like a brother to me so don't go round being a stranger naw." Miss Greene and everybody else around here just didn't seem to understand that I had nothing to share. How could they possibly understand what I'd been through? Simply, I came back home to forget and just start over. These people had spent all their lives complaining about the town yet never worked the courage up to cross the state line and see what else was out there. How could they understand the inner force that drove me to leave in search of something more than what they had to offer? And even worse the kind of pain and heartache that would send me back home? Like everything in life, this too eventually seemed to be passing by. They stopped coming over, asking questions or trying to get me out of the house. All that was left was the simple hellos and the talks behind my back.

Getting the house back in shape was my first project in hopes that would be enough to keep my mind occupied. There was so much to do and so much paperwork to deal with that I soon realized I was gonna have to hire some help. Looking through the classified section of the newspapers, I selected a few numbers, made a few phone calls, and finally went with a family-owned handyman/landscape company about thirty miles away from town. A middle-aged Mexican lady was sent from a cleaning agency to help out with the inside stuff. Pretty soon the stares and gossips were back again. Miss Greene came by asking me why I didn't ask the people around town for help, why she haven't seen me at church since I've been back, and indirectly how was I able to afford all this hired help. According to her, some were saying that my dad left me a large sum of insurance money. Others were saying that I made a lot of money in the big city and decided to come back to show it off but the most idiotic one was that I'd won the lottery. Miss. Greene, who strangely enough seemed more affected by these rumors, didn't seem to understand why I wasn't bothered by the gossips and the cold shoulders.

Spring went by and summer was coming to an end and most of the repairs around the house were complete and the freshly planted flowers added new life to the property. By the time the fall season rolled in, my hired help was gone and I was back to square one with my nostalgic thoughts, trying to figure out what to do. Nighttime was the worse. I'd crave company or someone to talk to. On few occasions the thought of calling Anthony or even Stanley crossed my mind but I never could go through with the idea. Thoughts of daddy would sometimes come fiercely through my head and bring me to tears and eminently thoughts of Deedee and Anthony would follow. On nights when I couldn't take it anymore, I would mix a screwdriver and my old Three Stooges video would come to the rescue.

By the time the yard and the house was what I wanted them to be, a little bit over a year had gone by. Most of that time went to working around the house, visiting the cemetery, and crying myself to sleep. I'm not sure what was holding me back. I just knew I wasn't yet ready to face the world at least not Savannah where everybody was waiting around to see what my next move was going to be.

I woke up one morning four years to the date when daddy was buried and decided I had enough. Sure I didn't become a lawyer but I had other skills I'm sure I could find something to do. The idea was to go take some flowers to the cemetery, then go downtown to fill out some job applications. I got dressed very quickly thinking I'd swing by the church for a quick prayer before heading for the cemetery. This way I'd have something good to tell daddy as I often sat and talked to him at the gravesite. It was the time of the morning where no one would be around to see me go into the church so I knew I didn't have to worry about having an audience.

The sanctuary was barely lit with the floor light illuminating the cross that was in on the back wall behind the pulpit and the sunshine peering through the stained glass windows. Coming from outside, it took me a few minutes for my eyes to adjust to the dimly lit room. I stood there looking around at the empty building and for some reason it seemed smaller than what I remembered. I walked slowly toward the front, touching every pew, remembering the days when me and daddy would sit in here listening to the many sermons which most of the time fell on deaf ears. I walked up to the third pew where daddy used to sit; I lowered myself onto the wooden bench and looked around as I fought back my tears. I was trying to remember what possessed me to come back here knowing how painful it would be. I felt like I should pray, asking Him why or what He wanted from me but words were too heavy to come out of my mouth. Instead the echoes of my cries just filled the room.

"We've missed your flowers around here." My cries died out into a quiet sob at the sound of the familiar voice. I quickly found some tissue out of my purse then turned around to find Rev. Myers coming towards me. "Rev Myers," I said, as I extended my hand towards him. "Sammie Lee" he said, ignoring my hand gesture and pulled me into a friendly hug. "How have you been? My wife and I have been praying for you." I looked down, embarrassed by the leftover tears on my face and said, "I'm sure I could use every bit of it." We sat down for a while reminiscing about the good old days; about daddy and the silly things he used to do, and how he used to brag about his vegetables. Rev. Myers told me about some of the church members that have died, those that got married and, of course, the grandkid's pictures that I couldn't escape. I was on my way out the door when I heard him say "I heard the flowers are looking pretty good this year." "They're getting there," I said. "Then I should be expecting a centerpiece for the Sunday service," he said. I quietly smiled and replied, "I'll see what I can do Reverend."

I wasn't yet ready to face the stares and the questions as before so Saturday afternoon; I got in the car and drove to Rev. Myers' to drop off the flowers for Sunday's service. I knew the Reverend would be at the church getting ready for tomorrow's service so the plan was to leave the flowers with his wife who wasn't much for talking. I knocked on the door for a while and gathered that she was probably at choir rehearsal, if things were still the same around here. I placed the arrangement on the cast iron table on the porch with a note explaining that I came by.

A few days later I was in the back working in the garden when I heard some-one at the front door. It was the Reverend and his wife coming by to thank me for the flowers. Pretty soon I was delivering flowers every Saturday for the Sun-day's service and by Christmas I was taking orders from the Reverend's wife for their daughter's engagement party. Instead of my personal life, my flowers were now the center of attention. My flowers were everywhere. At weddings, romantic dinners, birthday parties, hospitals and any other events or places. I finally felt redeemed.

Throughout the winter I had to either order the flowers from out of state or buy them from a warehouse near town but funny enough I enjoyed every bit of it. The idea of being able to bring some type of joy to these people gave me a sense of purpose and through no choice of my own I realized that I'd finally found my calling.

I was on my way to a job interview when I spotted this abandoned building. It was conveniently located on the riverbank between a bookstore and an opti-cal doctor's office. There was no sign to be found anywhere on or in the build-ing indicating what it used to be, but my mind could clearly see what it could become. I got out of the car to get a closer look at the inside through the win-dows, ignoring the fact that the time for my interview time was slipping by. "That would be the perfect place to open my flower shop," I thought. I just wish I knew whether it was on the market or not. I went towards the back. The small courtyard had a side view of the river, overgrown weeds and wild flowers and an old bench. I slowly lowered myself to the weathered bench, ignoring the fact that it could give in at any time when a slender version of Colonel Sanders called my attention over to my left on the backside of the optical office. "Can I help you with anything?" the older man asked. "I'm sorry," I said "I didn't mean to intrude…I was just looking around." He looked at me over his specta-cles, turned toward the riverbank and said, "It's beautiful here isn't it?" "It sure is." I replied still picturing my flower shop. "I've been here for fifteen years and this place still takes my breath away" he went on. "Sir?" I said moving closer to his building. "Sir, is not necessary," he said pushing his glasses further up his nose. "I know I'm old but folks around here call me Dr. Frank," he said, extending his hand towards me. "Nice meeting you Dr. Frank, I'm Leanne, would you happened to know who owns this building?" From what Dr. Frank told me the building had been unoccupied for more than a decade. It used to be a Hallmark store when he first transferred his office here but soon after, the owners moved out west. A landscape company comes by three to four times a year for the yard work but no one ever attempted to do anything with the place. Dr. Kurck gave me the name of the landscape company who tended to the yard and wished me luck before he went back to his duties. I rushed home, called where I was supposed to have the interview, apologized for not showing up, thanked them and told them that I accepted another position.

In little to no time, I found the landscaping company who was responsible for maintaining the property who then referred me to the owner. The property was in a cobweb of a family feud between an array of grandchildren who couldn't agree on what to do with the property that was left to them by their deceased grandmother. The sad part, according to the executor of the will, was the fact that all five parties involved were pretty well off. It was an ego fight more than anything else. The more I spoke to Mr. Johnston, the will executor, the more I realized that it really wasn't a matter of whether or not I could buy or lease the property it was just the fact that dealing with these people was to much of a hassle for him and therefore didn't want to deal with them. Normally, I would have probably let it go and looked for another place but for some reason, my heart was set on this place. It was so perfect for a flower shop. I kept calling Mr. Johnston and finally my persistence paid off. When he got back to me, his clients agreed to lease the property to me with the understanding that I would buy out the contract once they figured out whether they wanted to sell it or not or how much they wanted to sell it for. By then, my house and especially my dining room area had turned into a disaster zone with flowers, boxes, cards, ribbons and other miscellaneous items for my business to run. At first it wasn't so bad but then miraculously I landed a contract for a brand new hotel in town and realized that my business had taken over the house. My one-man show had sprouted overnight and it was obvious that I was gonna have to hire some help. I ran an ad in the local newspaper and hired a retired lady part time that was looking for something to do other then playing bingo and taking care of her dogs.

I took out a second mortgage on the house and the adjacent farm, used up all my life savings and finally I was able to move into my shop. The first few weeks were spent dealing with contractors, carpenters, painters and whoever else was necessary to get the shop in running condition.

CHAPTER 19

It was a few months after the engagement and Abigail was now pressing Anthony to set a date for the wedding. Anthony did everything he could to avoid the topic because although he didn't have a problem being engaged, he just couldn't see himself married to Abigail or anyone at this point in his life. Of course, he loved Abigail, but the same reasons he loved her as a girlfriend were the same reasons he couldn't see her as a wife. Things like not wanting children, her wanting to move to Chicago when her job relocated in the upcoming year and so many other reasons, as far as Anthony was concerned, Abigail was already married to her job and he couldn't see her changing for anybody. For the past few months every time she'd press him about the wedding date, he'd find himself strangely enough thinking about Samantha. At first he thought it was just old memory surfacing because of his apprehension about marrying Abigail but as time went by, even little things of the past like a smell, a song or sometime a location would take him back to thoughts of him and Samantha. Andrew suggested that Anthony break up with Abigail and move on with his life but Anthony didn't see this as a solution because after all he loved Abigail, they were great as a couple and he didn't want to lose her. He just didn't want to marry her. The thoughts of Samantha were nothing else but THOUHTS after all she was one of the longest relationships he ever had. What he needed to do was to figure out a way to make Abigail happy without compromising what he wanted and so reluctantly he asked her to move in with him.

Anthony was finally on vacation after a long trail of intensive cases that had been consuming his life. Abigail, who was supposed to be off at the same time, was suddenly called back to work to meet some deadline that someone else couldn't pull through and as a result their cruise to the Virgin Islands had to be cancelled. The tickets were non-refundable so rather than letting them go to waste Abigail suggested to gift them to her parents. Anthony had been to the Virgin Islands a thousand times, so he really didn't mind. He was just disappointed that most of his vacation would go by without him seeing his girlfriend.

Abigail's parents came down a week before the trip to visit and spend some time with their daughter and Abigail insisted that Anthony spent some time with them since she would be working during the day. Although Anthony had met them before he never realized how much they were like their daughter. All they did was talk about themselves and wedding plans for Abigail and Anthony. Two days was all it took for him to change his vacation plans and head for London. Anthony wasn't in London for more than a couple of days when Stanley informed him that he would be traveling back to the States to assist one of their clients.

The sun was finally shining my way, things were coming along smoothly, business was coming in, I finally managed to turn part of the ten-acres adjacent to the house into a nursery with a small crew just enough to support some of the demands of the store. Marie, my part-time worker at the store, turned out to be very dependable and a productive worker who insisted on fatting me up by consistently bringing me some of the best home cooked dishes on the pretense that they were leftovers on their way to the trash. The biggest turn around of it all is how the town had finally decided to take me in as their own just as I was.

Almost a year after opening the store, I received a certified letter from Mr. Johnston's law firm stating in so many words that there was some problems with the title of the property and that I had ninety days to evacuate the shop. When I finally got a hold of Johnston, he tried to explain to me that due to circumstances, my contract would be void and there was a good chance that I would also lose the money that I'd invested in the property. The whole time I was thinking "you gotta be shitting me, after all the money I've invested in this place now they pull this shit." The worst part about it is the fact that they didn't even want to work with me, they were just being mean-spirited about the whole thing. I looked up a few law firms around town and started calling around. They were charging an arm and a leg for their services because they were so many parties involved. After days and nights torn up about the whole dilemma I decided to call Stanley and see if I could get some legal counsel and perhaps I might be able to take care of it by myself. It'd been almost two years since I'd spoken to Stanley so the whole concept of calling him was somewhat unnerving. I wasn't sure if I wanted to go down that path because it had been a long and painful road, I was finally getting on with my life and now it felt like the only way I could save my future was to go back into my past.

Ever since his retirement, Stanley had been spending most of his time in London keeping an eye on the firm and cherry-picking a couple of cases a year to work so I knew I had a fair chance at getting a hold of him at his London's home. I was so nervous that I decided to call when he would least likely be home this way I could leave a message and the decision would be his whether he wanted to call me back or not.

Wednesdays were his golfing days so on Tuesday, I woke up a nervous wreck in the middle of the night trying to figure out what I was gonna say to Stanley. What do you say to someone that you haven't spoken to in almost two years, someone who'd been nothing but kind to you and just like that you disappear out of their lives and now here I was calling them after all this time asking them for help. Finally 3:00 A.M. my time, I picked up the phone with sweaty palms and dialed the number. The minute the answering machine picked up my mind froze and for the first time I realized that Stanley's voice was a more mature version of Anthony's. A few seconds after the beep I finally worked up the nerve to let the words out of my mouth and after leaving a brief message I quickly hung up and spent the rest of the day questioning myself whether I should of called or not.

A couple of days went by, I was in the middle of a transaction when I heard Marie on the phone trying to tell someone on the other end that there was nobody by the name of Samantha working here. As soon as I heard the name Samantha, I excused myself and rushed to grab the phone out of her hands and asked her to finish taking care of the customer. I picked up the phone and sure enough it was Stanley. He sounded so happy to hear from me that all my apprehension slowly disappeared and suddenly it felt like the prodigal child returning home. We stayed on the phone awhile playing catch up and by the time I got done explaining the nature of the situation of the shop, it felt just like old times. I really wanted to ask and find out how Anthony was doing but I didn't want to cross that line. Hesitantly, I heard myself asking how the boys were doing. Stanley must have read in between the lines and started telling me about Anthony. Before they hung up, per my request, Stanley promised not to let the boys know that we'd made contact and he informed me that he was planning to come to the states in a couple of weeks for a trip to Chicago. He said on his way back from his trip, he would stop by and handle the legal issues in question. The next few days that followed, I felt like a load had been lifted off my shoulders. Calling Stanley was a hard decision for me but now with him in the picture, I felt certain that things would work out in my favor. My only downfall was the fact that thoughts of Anthony, which I'd worked hard to put behind me, were now coming back. This was the last thing I needed right now with everything going on so I went back to focusing on the things that mattered most for the moment, the store.

It was 11:30 A.M. on a Monday morning when Anthony made it to Savannah, Georgia. As he drove around the streets in his rental car, his mind was wondering where his dad had gotten a client from this town. He'd been in the firm long enough where he thought he knew most, if not all the clients that his father dealt with, but for some reason the name Leanne Harper didn't seem to ring a bell. Anthony followed the pre-written directions to Johnston's law firm to discuss Leanne Harper's case. It didn't take him long to realize that the couple of days in and out plan that he envisioned was going to take much longer. His next stop was at the flower shop to meet with his client, Ms. Harper. As he drove around taking in the peacefulness and welcoming feel of the town, he tried to picture what his client would be like. Being one of his dad's client and with such a mature name, he pictured a widow in her late fifties, the perfect grandmotherly type who probably spent most of her time at the store and baked cookies for the neighborhood kids on the weekend.

Minutes later, Anthony walked through the glass door of the flower shop. As he watched Marie box the long stem roses for a blonde-haired woman, he trapped a smile on his face at the thought of his accurate perception of whom he believed to be Leanne. Marie said hello and told him she'd be right with him. As he waited, Anthony walked around the store looking at the arrangement displays, flowers in a double door glassed freezer, some of which he'd never seen before. He thought about sending some flowers to Abigail but the thought quickly left his mind as he pictured them dying on a table before she could take the time from work to enjoy them or even look at them. As the customer headed out the door with obvious satisfaction, Anthony extended his hand as he walked up to Marie.

"Ms. Leanne Harper, I'm Anthony Wellington. I'm here to handle…" "Oh dear one," Marie laughed cutting in before he could finish "this is definitely one of the nicest compliments you could lay on an old lady but unfortunately I can't take the credit for being Leanne. I'm probably old enough to be Leanne's grandmother and I'm sure she's at least twice as beautiful as I am. She won't be here for awhile; this is her day to be at the nursery, was she expecting you?"

"Actually no," Anthony said, "I had a slight change of plans. I was supposed to come in tomorrow, but no worries. Do you know when she'll be back?" According to Marie, Leanne was supposed to call her and let her know when she would be coming to the shop but being that she was at the nursery that could be any time. By then Anthony was ready for lunch so he asked Marie for some recommendations for a few nearby places where he could grab a bite and told her he'd stop by again on the way to his hotel.

When Samantha made it back to the store, it was way past time for Marie to go feed her dogs. She told Samantha about all the messages that were on her desk and quickly left for the day. By the time Samantha finished the last few orders it was time for her to close. Without checking her desk she went to the back room to the fridge for her Thursday check up routine since Marie usually left her some of her best so called leftover cooked meals.

CHAPTER 20

Fridays were my busiest and favorite days at the shop. Most people needed flowers on Fridays either for a celebration, a date, a dinner party or many other things that seemed to always take place over the weekend. I was in the backroom of the shop going over some paperwork with the delivery guy and Marie was in the front tending to a customer when the chiming of the bells indicated that someone had either left or entered the shop. The gaily greetings from Marie that were soon followed confirmed the latter.

"Hi, how are you liking Savannah so far?" she asked. "Very nice madam, is Ms Harper here today?" asked the newcomer. "She sure is, she had such a long day yesterday that she didn't even get a chance to go through her messages but I'm sure she won't mind seeing you." As I halfway listened to Marie, I wondered how many times I've asked her to stop putting my business out in the street. The problem with Marie, like everybody else in this town, is that they talked too damn much but you couldn't help but love Marie. She was like the mother I never had, always telling me how I was working too hard, not eating right and on a few occasions how I needed a man in my life. Sometimes I had to remind myself that she was working for me instead of the other way around.

"Leanne there's a nice young man out here to see you." Marie came out back to tell me. "Is there a problem?" I asked her quietly because usually she deals with the customers when I'm busy in the back, whether she heard me or not she didn't answer. So I followed her footsteps to the front. As if seeing a ghost, we both froze in the moment unable to believe our eyes. "Leanne," Marie looked at me and said, "this is Anthony Wellington. He came by to see you yesterday while you were at the nursery." Then turning to Anthony she said, "See I told you she was twice as beautiful as me." "I can see that," he said looking at

Marie with his cunning yet honest signature smile that I'd spent these past years forgetting. He turned toward me and extended his hand for a shake. I nervously met his hand with mine as I tried to bring my thoughts back together. He looked painfully good in his black suit. "I didn't realize that Stanley…I mean your father wasn't able to make it." I forced myself to say. Still looking at me he said, "Change of plans, I guess." Feeling the uncomfortable stare from Marie and our customer, I asked her to finish with the customer while I tended to Mr. Wellington.

Anthony followed me into the small office and closed the door behind us. My stomach leaped into a long drop before a crash landing but I kept my features cool and composed; at least I tried to as I turned to face him. There was an awkward silence between us both unsure of what to say. "How's everybody doing?" I asked when I was able to speak again. He spoke slowly and said, "Everyone is…well…, I'm still getting over the fact that I'm standing here with you…" "That makes two of us." I take it that your father didn't tell you?" I asked softly. "You're correct," he responded, as he ran his hand through his hair, a sign that used to mean that he was gathering his thoughts. "I don't know what to make of this," he said conversationally, "you walked out of my life and here you are with a new name…" "Look," I cut in before he could say anything else "I did not walk out on you and I especially don't need you to come here passing judgment on me about my name or anything else, clearly calling your father was a mistake so feel free to get back on your high horse and leave at your convenience." I moved from the far side of the room toward the door but he beat me to it. "Wait," he said, stopping me in my tracks "you got to give me some lenience here; there's no reason to let our past stop us from working together. I had no idea I was gonna run into you but I did promise to handle your case, so at least let me do that." Silence filled the room again, if it wasn't for the audience being in the front room I would of stormed right out of the store but Anthony was right. There was no reason why we couldn't put our past aside and focus on the case, especially when my deadline was so near. I just didn't realize how hard it was gonna be.

I drove home that night replaying the events of the day. All I could think about was Anthony. Upon his estimation everything would be settled by the end of the following week, that meant I'd be dealing with him for the next eight days, which to me was an eternity. How was I supposed to function with him looking so painfully good? He was never the kind that anyone could ignore physically, so I knew it was gonna take more than strong will to keep him out of my mind or me falling for him again. I worked myself crazy day and night, arranged for all of our meetings and phone calls to be in the store just to eliminate the possibility of my being alone or having him come by my house. Despite my effort, every time he came by the store, it was like a replay of the pain of me losing him all over again.

Every once in a while he'd throw me a curve ball and surprise me with a question about my being here, leaving without saying goodbye, about my name or why I wouldn't let him know where I lived. It'd take every bit of my strength to brush him off when deep down I wished I could just forget about everything and tell him what he wanted to know about my past, my life now in Georgia and the truth about how I felt about him. But what would be the point? To be rejected and go through the heartache all over again? Anthony was done with everything by Thursday. Friday right before noon, Marie left early to pick up her daughter from the airport leaving me solo at the store. Minutes later Anthony walked in the store with a big smile on his face, the kind that brought back a lot of good old memories. "I missed you yesterday," he greeted me. "I had a few things to do at the nursery," I responded. "That's what Marie told me," he said approaching my front desk. "Did you hear the good news?" "I sure did," I responded unable to keep a straight face "I don't know how I'll ever repay you." "Well," he quickly responded "you could go out and celebrate with me for a start." "Tempting," I responded smiling at his enthusiasm "but as you can see Marie's not here and I can't afford to close the store if I'm to pay your legal fees," I joked. "I'm sure we can make some arrangements for the fees," he said teasingly, "besides by law you're allowed at least a thirty minute lunch break." He looked so amazing that it took all my strength to fight back the constant impulses that had been roaming through my head, hoping this was nothing more than sexual lust. After all he was engaged and was no longer mine to fantasize about. "I'm sorry Anthony, I just don't wanna complicate things." He looked at me for a moment as if taken in what I said, then suddenly he got this up to no good look on his face and said, "I'll be right back," as he rushed out the door. Half and hour later, Anthony came back with a basket packed with lunch saying "having lunch at the store is not too complicated is it?" Before I could give him an answer, he placed the basket on the counter, looking through it he said "we got your favorite roast beef with provolone, light mayo and mustard, Baked Lays, wine and" pausing for a more dramatic affect, "oatmeal raisin cookies." I opened my mouth to throw him an excuse and realized that nothing I could say would deter him in anyway so I had to admit defeat. I laughed, amazed that he remembered so much and thankful that the store was empty. I put the "Out to Lunch" sign up and headed outside to the courtyard. I'd forgotten how nice it was to sit out in the sun. Everything seemed so peaceful. The riverbank glistened in small ripples, the trees and grass moved lazily to the soft rhythm of the wind. We sat comfortably on the old bench that had recently been repaired, enjoying the breeze. There was a familiar air around us as we ate and talked about old times, stories about Andrew, the guys at the firm, Stanley and even Deedee, no mentioning of what could have or should have been just two old friends enjoying a pleasant lunch. We were both laughing about something silly when suddenly we both stopped as if on cue. He looked at me intently and said, "How are you really doing?" This was the million dollar question which had it been asked a year ago I probably could have listed a ton of things that needed to be dealt with and here I was sitting next to Anthony of all people. I thought for a second at the irony of it all, let out a heavy breath and said "a lot better now." I was thinking of other things to say but he spoke before I had a chance to. "I looked all over for you after you left…I missed you." His words caught me off guard, tighten up my chest with emotion. Neither one of us moved I wanted to turn and face him but I didn't dare. It felt so good to hear those words out of his mouth but didn't know what to say. An awkward silence was starting to creep up on us so I quickly said, "Enough about me what about you? I guess congratulations on your engagement are in order." I regretted the words the moment they came out of my mouth. Why the hell did I bring that up? I bit the lower part of my lip, wishing I could take the words back. "I see my father has been spilling the dirt on me, so what else did he tell you?" I let out an easy laugh to cover up my discomfort, "Other than the fact that you got engaged, not much." I replied. There were no more jokes or laughter, his smile faded slowly as he repeated the words "engaged," paused for a second then talking more to himself he said, "That was a mistake on my part."

This was the kind of comment that was best left alone so I quickly tried to merge into safer ground. "What about Trudy? What is she up to these days?" The grateful smile that was now on his face spoke louder than words. We were safely back on neutral ground talking about things that didn't make neither one of us uncomfortable. As we finished the rest of the wine, my mind went back and forth between listening to him telling me about Trudy, memories of us, and my present feelings towards him. Almost an hour went by without us knowing it and I had to force myself to get back to work. "I think my lunch break is over," I said getting off the bench. "You only have two days left so I'm sure you'd like to relax, do a few attractions before you head back to the big city." He got up without saying a word, his lanky body towering over me.

"Thanks for everything," I said looking up at him. He smiled a gentle smile that warmed me up all over and said, "It felt good to see you again." Then pulled me into a big bear hug before saying goodbye.

CHAPTER 21

⚜

The whole deal with Mr. Johnston turned out to be a fraud. Everything from the grandchildren's stories, to the contract being defaulted. The only intention Mr. Johnston ever had was to take me and my money for a ride.

He and his associate apparently owned various condemned properties all over Georgia and the Carolinas. They lured small businesses and private investors into renovating their properties. All accounts were managed by his firm so that all transactions would be written out to his firm then purposely defaulted the contract by depositing mortgage or lease payments into an account that could not be traced to the property. Once the contract goes into default, the investor ended up losing whatever time and money put into the properties. Johnston and his firm concentrated in small enough towns so the odds of the investors fighting back would be slim to none. What he didn't bet on was for a lonesome 5'7" woman to fight back.

The days between Tuesday and Friday I did fine avoiding Anthony's off topic questions and any kind of feelings toward him that were trying to surface, then came Saturday. I was about to get in my car after closing the shop, when Anthony pulled into the parking lot. Wondering what would put him in such a rush I pushed the door shut and wished it wouldn't be bad news of some sort. The unhurried movement from his car told me that it couldn't be that serious. "I was hoping I'd catch you before you closed," he said as he got near me. "Is everything okay?" I asked. "Everything's fine" he said still moving towards me, "I just wanted to see if you had any plans for the night since it is my first and last weekend in Georgia. I thought we could spend it together."

"I'm sorry," I lied, looking down at my keys. "I really have a lot to do, maybe next time." "How about tomorrow?" he persisted, "Marie invited me to a Sunday brunch that her church is having. She's very fond of you so I'm sure she wouldn't mind you coming along." "And I'm sure her and everybody else there won't mind playing the 20 questions game about my showing up with you either. I'm sorry but my life is not open for review."

"Kind of like it was with me, eh?" he said slowly. Everything I'd been holding in just came flooding back. I hated him for bringing this into the conversation. Every inch of my body tensed up and it had nothing to with my day's work. "What's that suppose to mean?" I halfway shouted. "Samantha," he said calmly, "the least you could do is..." "The least I could do is what?" I cut in before he could finish. "I don't owe you a thing. I've paid a great deal and apologized enough for my mistakes. I'm tired of trying to make amends. If you can't forgive me then that's on you." I spun around to get to my car door wishing that my words didn't come out so breathy, or showing how much of an impact he had on me especially when he on the other hand seemed so calm and controlled. He reached over my shoulder for the door and said as he grabbed my hand "I'm not asking for an apology." I turned to look at him momentarily speechless and finally said, "Then what the hell do you want from me?" He took a couple of steps closing in the space between us and said, "To learn about the girl I fell in love with." His voice quivered with undertone and before I could answer I was trapped by his beautiful lips over mine.

I drove home barely aware of my surroundings trying to figure out what just happened. I can't believe I let him kiss me, what was I thinking? The man's engaged to be married and here I was melting at the memory of his lips. I sank into my living room couch trying to compose my thoughts. I kept telling myself, "This can't be happening, I can't go back down that path." Despite the logic of why I shouldn't want him and knowing of the pain that would follow if I didn't snap out of this, I couldn't ignore the cravings that I'd been holding back since Tuesday morning when I laid eyes on him. I wished he was the kind that could be physically ignored. That would make things a whole lot easier.

These were the moments when I wished I had someone to talk to and missed Deedee the most. She would have told me to stop thinking, have fun and worry about the consequences later. But then that's probably why she wasn't...I couldn't finish that thought; old pain and sadness were now swelling up in my throat. Suddenly the house was too quiet; I turned on the TV and soon realized that neither The Three Stooges nor the local channels would do it for the night. A couple of shots of Tequila would probably do the trick but I'd clean out the cupboards in my attempt to sober up. I looked at the clock it wasn't yet 8:00 P.M., too early to go to bed. I took a quick shower, quickly got dress grabbed my keys and headed out the door.

Unlike my mind, the night was still and full of moonlight. I drove passed the two local bars thinking that the 10:00 P.M. closing kind of bar where most people would know me would not do. I had to go into town.

I found a bar and took refuge in a dark corner with a beer. With a football game going on, most of the customers were hugging up the space in front of the TV cheering on the game. I tuned out the noise and tried to focus on the things that were roaming through my head. I went back and forth with my thoughts and the more I thought about things, the more evident it was that I still loved him. By the end of the night, I decided I was gonna go to the brunch the next day and tell him how I felt about him. I know he was engaged but it's not like I'm asking him to leave his girlfriend. I just needed to get this off my chest.

Sunday morning I got up and headed for the brunch. I don't know what I was expecting or if I even had any expectations. It just felt good to finally listen to my heart. The church's front yard was lined up with cars and full of noise from the crowd of people that filled the yard and the picnic tables. I looked around hoping to spot his car but gave up when I saw Marie coming towards me. The smell of the grill hit me before I could reach Marie by the oversized flagpoles, "Hey Leanne, what a nice surprise. I'm glad you changed your mind about joining us." She hugged me hello and instantly dragged me into the crowds introducing me to people that I'd met and some that I'd previously seen at the shop or around town. I absentmindedly said hello as I visually patrolled the surroundings.

Everybody was going around eating, playing, and chatting while my heart was cringing with nervousness. I roamed around with a glass of lemonade hoping that he was just running late. "He's not coming," said a voice coming from behind me. It was Marie, she must have snuck up on me because I didn't even hear her coming. "What are you talking about?" I said trying to pretend it didn't matter. "I was young once, believe it or not, and it didn't take much for me to figure out that there was history between y'all..., you two making out yesterday just confirmed it." "I was not making out with him" I softly exclaimed. "It's okay," she whispered "I'm not judging you, I would be all over him too if I was twenty years younger."

There was no point in pretending about Anthony or trying to figure out how my kissing him got around town so quickly. I let out an easy breath, forced a smile on my face and asked, "How do you know he's not coming? Did he say something to you?" She hooked her arm into mine and led me away from the crowd.

"He came by earlier this morning on his way to the airport," she replied. "The airport?" I repeated in disbelieve "I thought he wasn't supposed to leave until tomorrow morning." She must have heard the disappointment in my voice. We were both silent for a moment then with her free hand she padded my arm and asked if I was gonna be okay? I didn't have a choice but to be. I knew he was just passing through; I just didn't realized how much his leaving without saying goodbye would affect me. I turned to look at her and said, "Would you mind…?" I didn't need to finish she knew exactly what I wanted to say. "It's okay dear I understand, go home and I'll see you tomorrow." I freed my hand from hers and started to leave when she said "Wait I have something for you in my car." I followed her to her station wagon where she handed me an envelope and said "He asked me to give this to you." I took the envelope with a pounding heart hugged her and drove away.

I drove home feeling like a child waking up from a deep sleep to find out she had missed Christmas. The difference was there would always be next year for Christmas. In my case, I didn't know. I pulled into my driveway and ran into the house anxious to find out the content of the envelope. Sitting on the couch I tore open the envelope and there was a gift and a note. The note said, "Dear Samantha, I have to go home and sort out my feelings after seeing you. I need to make some decisions about a lot of things before I can move forward. Sorry to leave you like this. Forever, Anthony"

It felt like I was going to go back into that deep depression, it's as if I lost him all over again. Part of me wondered why I didn't trust my heart. Part of me was mad for letting him slip away one more time and the other part of me was mad for not being over him. I was mopping around for days after he left unable to get him out of my mind. The note that he left me was a constant reminder of my confusion. I didn't know what he was trying to say or what I was supposed to even read into it.

Marie kept hinting around trying to get me to talk about things but I was so confused I didn't know where to start or what to say. The only thing I knew for sure was the fact that I was heart broken and I didn't even know why. I knew he wasn't mine and logically I knew I should get over him and move on but my heart didn't want to let go.

The following week after Anthony left, Marie and I were sitting in the back-room drinking coffee while going over the books before we opened up, when Marie looked up and said, "That's it, I'm tired of you mopping around you need to do something about this." "I'm fine…," I started to say but she grabbed my hand which forced me to look at her. "I've asked you a question three times and I bet you can't even tell me what it was." "I'm sorry Marie, my mind is just…I don't know. So what was your question?" "It's not important," she sat back, still looking at me and said, "So what's going on with you two?" "What do you mean?" I asked as I painted a smile on my face. "I've been watching you be miserable since he left." "Obviously you still love him, so what are you gonna do?" "I'm not sure there's anything I can do." I said looking down into my coffee cup. "Leanne," she called my name forcing me to look back up at her and said, "don't let your past take away your happiness." "You make it sound so easy," I told her, "I had my chance and I screwed it up. When I should have fought for him I didn't. It's like crying over spilled milk," the words weighted like lead. "He's engaged anyway, so what's the point? What I need to do is get over him." "The point is, it's never too late until they both say I do. Do you still love him?" she asked. Without hesitation I heard myself say, "I do, I do love him." For the first time I allowed these words to be spoken out loud and it felt real good. "Then," she said now holding on to my hand "the question should be how are you gonna get him back?"

Marie wasn't the kind to be so assertive so it was surprising for me to hear her talk like that. She freed my hand and I grabbed my cup of coffee for a sip. "From what I understand," she said slowly, "his girlfriend's moving to Chicago." I raised my eyebrow at her in puzzlement. Reading the confusion on my face she explained, "He mentioned something along those lines Sunday morning when he dropped by so I added two and two together." I wondered what he must have said because I know Anthony wasn't the kind to share things about his personal life.

I'm not sure why but I reached for my purse, pulled out Anthony's note that I'd been carrying around with me since he left and handed it to Marie. As she read the note, I let out a heavy breath and said, "What if he doesn't love me anymore?" When she was done reading she looked up at me, slid me back the note and the phone that had been resting on the table and without blinking her eyes she said, "And what if he does?" She got out of her chair handed me the phone that had been resting on the table and walked out of the room.

CHAPTER 22

Before I could change my mind, my fingers quickly dialed his numbers from memory. I wasn't sure what I was going to say but somehow I was disappointed when his voicemail picked up.

Thank God for Fridays. With everything to be done before the weekend, I barely had time to tend to my heart so it wasn't until later that night that I started wondering whether or not he'd gotten my message, if he was gonna call me, or if my calling him was a mistake.

I had just put on my favorite episode of The Three Stooges before going into the kitchen for a glass of lemonade when I heard the knock on the front door. Already back to the ways of my hometown where most front doors were left unlocked I called out from the kitchen to come in as I placed the lemonade container back in the fridge. I carried my glass to the front room and found myself dumbfounded at the sight of Anthony in the middle of my living room. "An-tho-ny?" "Samantha!" As if we'd both seen a ghost, we blurted out each other's name at the same time as I watched my glass of lemonade fall out of my hand. We both went for the glass but not fast enough. Hunched over the broken glass we were both silent for a moment unable to think of the right words to say. "What are you doing here?" I asked when I finally found my voice. "I probably should have called first but you never gave me your number and," he said brushing his hand through his hair, "I needed to see you." That still didn't answer how he found me but I had more pressing things to deal with right now. "Did you get my message?" I asked. "I didn't know you called," he said raising his eyebrows in puzzlement. "I've been at the airport all afternoon trying to catch a flight and I hope you're not too upset with my showing up here unannounced." He pulled me up and moved us away from the lemonade and broken glass. "I broke off the engagement," he said, now standing in the living room. "She wanted something I wasn't ready to give and I got tired of measuring her up to you. It wasn't fair to neither one of us." He took a brief pause then went on, "I know there is a lot that needs to be worked out but I'd like another chance at us. I meant what I said Saturday, I want to know the girl I fell in love with." "That could take a while," I said. "I got a lifetime," he replied, "would that do?" I briefly closed my eyes to make sure I wasn't dreaming. At this point I didn't care how he found me I was just happy to have another chance at us. When I opened my eyes they were full of tears but this time they were tears of joy. I extended my hand and hoarsely whispered, "Hi, I'm Samantha Leanne Goldsmith, I was born here in Savannah Georgia in…" He pulled me toward him and lowered us to the couch. My lips opened in invitation as his tongue penetrated the depth of my mouth. I was pressed against his chest with his arms around me and the only thought running through my head was how much I wanted him. As he nibbled on my ears, every part of my body went weightless emphasizing the throbbing warmth between my inner thighs. I pried myself out of his arms and pulled him up to me and said, "I do have a bed." "Lead the way," he whispered in my ears. Obviously my life story was gonna have to wait for some other time. There were other things that couldn't wait a lifetime and making love was one of them.

CHAPTER 23

The tickle in the back of my neck from his even breathing woke me up the next morning. I smiled happily, taking it all in, enjoying the warmth of his skin against mine. I eased out of his arms to open the windows, careful not to wake him. The flowers beds that ran from the back patio all the way to the nursery path were waking up to the new coming sun. I closed my eyes as the morning air brushed on my face then felt his body behind me. He pulled me into his arms and wrapped me into the sheet that covered him. "I didn't mean to wake you up," I said softly. He smiled a gently and said, "I was missing you." His manhood that now stood at attention against me was enough supporting evidence of his claim. "Will I have to farm to live here?" he said teasingly in between kisses on my face as he looked out the window. "You can if you want but I think starting a firm in Savannah will be more than enough to keep you occupied. We stayed at the window for a while pointing and naming the flowers from where we stood. As the sun sailed silently higher, we talked about me, the old me and the new, when the new Wellington's firm could open in Savannah, rearranging the house to make room for his stuff, my future father and brother-in-law and whatever else we could think of. We did have more than a plate full to work on but what does it matter when you have a lifetime ahead of you.

The End

978-0-595-39152-3
0-595-39152-4

Printed in the United States
51327LVS00003B/166